BOOMERANG

The happy camaraderie of the Porth-cove Studios holiday hotel is shattered by the arrival of the misanthropic George Bullard. He goes out of his way to annoy both staff and fellow artist guests. So when Bullard is found brutally murdered, everyone in the hotel comes under suspicion as having a motive to kill him. Then there is a second murder . . . The police are baffled, and it falls to the unorthodox lady detective Miss Isabel Eaton to unmask the killer.

SYDNEY J. BOUNDS

BOOMERANG

Complete and Unabridged

LINFORD
Leicester

First published in Great Britain

First Linford Edition
published 2008

British Library CIP Data

Bounds, Sydney J.
  Boomerang.—Large print ed.—
  Linford mystery library
  1. Detective and mystery stories
  2. Large type books
  I. Title
  823.9'14 [F]

  ISBN 978–1–84782–256–7

Published by
F. A. Thorpe (Publishing)
Anstey, Leicestershire

Set by Words & Graphics Ltd.
Anstey, Leicestershire
Printed and bound in Great Britain by
T. J. International Ltd., Padstow, Cornwall

1

Unpleasantness At Porthcove

George Bullard breezed into Porthcove, whistling an old-fashioned tune. He was starting two weeks' holiday and intended to enjoy every minute of it. Even if some other people didn't.

He swung his Volvo across the road and into the driveway under a sign that read Porthcove Studios and braked in front of a large house built of grey stone. The house was old with a new extension added at the seaward end and a broad expanse of lawn. There was a pond in the centre of the lawn.

Three people stood in the shade of the front porch. The welcoming committee, Bullard thought as he got out. A late afternoon sun still blazed over the clifftops and he could smell the sea below.

A small man with plain features stepped into the sunlight. 'I'll help with

1

your luggage and park your car.'

Bullard tossed him the keys. 'Fine. I've always wanted a slave.'

The woman holding a clip-board frowned slightly. 'I'm Val Courtney. And you are — ?'

'George Bullard. The one and only.'

'Welcome, Mr. Bullard, and I hope you'll enjoy your stay with us. You're in room number two. My husband, Reggie, will show you the way.'

'The accommodation is first class, I hope? And the food too — I warn you, I'm first class at complaining.'

Bullard dumped a large suitcase on the ground and followed that with a folding easel, a box of paints and an assortment of primed canvases.

'If you damage anything,' he said cheerfully. 'I'll sue.'

The third person moved leisurely out of the porch. He was slender with blond hair and a silk scarf at his throat and moved like a dancer.

'I'd like to introduce your tutor for the course.' Val said. 'Keith Parry.'

'Never heard of him. Not an R.A., are you?'

Parry said calmly, 'You're right, I'm not.'

Bullard turned to Reg Courtney and snapped his fingers. 'All right, let's get organized. Forward march!'

Reggie picked up the heavy suitcase and led the way and Bullard followed with his painting gear. Beyond the front door was a hall with a pay-phone and stairs leading to the upper part of the house.

Reggie went through a doorway on the right. 'This is the common room.'

There were armchairs grouped about a large television set and a pile of art magazines on a table.

Reggie opened the far door leading to the new annexe and struggled down a passage with the suitcase. Bullard strolled along behind, smiling to himself.

The door of the first room stood open and another holiday painter was sorting through his equipment.

Bullard paused in the doorway and glared at a man with swarthy skin and a hooked nose.

'Don't tell me,' he said loudly. 'I've

been put next to a ruddy jewboy!' His voice held a cutting edge of contempt. 'What are you selling, Ikey? Never mind the cut, feel the quality — I'll complain to the management.'

The jew turned to face Bullard.

'Schmuck!' he exclaimed, and slammed the door.

George Bullard chuckled.

Reggie said, without expression, 'You'll have to see Val if you want another room.'

'Don't bother. I'm going to have some fun with our sheeny friend.'

Reggie carried the suitcase into room number two.

Bullard paused in the doorway, sniffing the air. 'What, no air-conditioning?' He put down his gear, opened the window and looked out at the garden.

'Bathroom at the end of the passage,' Reggie said. 'Dinner's at seven. To reach the dining room, go back to the hall and turn right — it's the first door on the left.'

After Reggie had gone, Bullard soaked in the bath and changed into casual clothes. He took his time arriving at the dining room; he'd found, on similar occasions, that he could upset staff and disrupt service by being deliberately late.

He heard a cheerful chatter as the other painters in the party introduced themselves. When he strolled in, he saw there were two tables; a long one for the students and a second, smaller table placed close to the kitchen door for Val, her husband and the tutor.

The jew sat next to a tall man with cropped greying hair. There was a young and pretty blonde in jeans and tee-shirt with a surly youth wearing a leather jacket. And a middle-aged woman with long black hair, brass earrings and a gaudy dress.

Bullard said, 'Hello, hello, hello. What's for dinner?' He wrinkled his nose. 'Not fish?'

'Local fish,' Val Courtney said. 'Fresh today.'

'I've heard that one before.' Bullard said loudly. 'Fresh from the fridge!'

'And the salad is grown in our own garden.'

'Salad? Rabbit food — never touch it.'

'If you'll state your requirements,' Val

said coldly, 'I'll arrange it. We try to please everyone.'

'Steak. With jacket potatoes.'

'Very well, Mr. Bullard. It would help if you could be on time for meals as we've only a small staff.'

She went into the kitchen to speak to the cook.

After dinner, Keith Parry stood up. 'We'll all meet in the studio — it's opposite, just across the passage — for an introductory chat.'

As they left the dining room, Bullard spoke to the tall man. 'I'd recognise that accent anywhere. Australian, aren't you?'

'Right on, mate. Fletcher's the name.'

'Bullard. I imagine your grandparents were convicts then? Botany Bay, and all that. Do they still flog prisoners down under?'

Fletcher said, 'Up yours, Jack,' and walked away.

'George, not Jack, old boy.'

Grinning, George Bullard entered the studio. It was a long room containing easels and stools, each with a rest for a drawing board. In one corner was an electric kiln, and an unfinished mosaic lay spread out on a table.

Keith Parry said, 'Please leave the kiln alone, Mr. Bullard, I'm firing clay tesserae as an experiment.'

Gradually, the holiday painters gathered. Val Courtney brought in coffee on a tray and went out again.

Parry said, briskly: 'Everyone settled? Good. First of all, I'm Keith. I hope we'll all be on first name terms — it's so much friendlier, I feel.'

Bullard leered. 'Especially with the ladies.'

'I want each of you to enjoy these two weeks, to leave here having made new friends and learnt something. Now I'd like you to introduce yourselves and tell me what medium you're using.'

Bullard got in first.

'I'm George, and I paint in oils — the only possible medium for any serious painter. I'm good. If you're busy, Keith, I can help out.'

'I don't think that will be necessary . . . and ladies first, please.'

The pretty blonde girl said eagerly,

'Linda. I've brought water colours, but I'm a complete beginner. This is the first time I've been on a sketching holiday.'

'Then I'll give you extra attention.'

'Me too,' Bullard said.

Parry ignored him. 'Does your boy-friend paint, Linda?'

'No, Duke's just keeping me company. I was too nervous to come here on my own.'

'You won't be on your own for long,' Bullard said with a smirk.

The woman who looked like a gypsy said, 'Margo. I like to use a mixture of different media — crayons and ballpoints and wash and well, just any old thing that comes to hand. Chalk and pencil and the end of a brush dipped in ink.'

'Yes, it's possible to get some interesting effects that way.'

'Call me Jim,' the Australian drawled. 'I do a bit of everything, but it's mainly drawing that interests me.'

'Fine, Jim.'

'Sammy,' the jew said. 'I paint in oils too and I want to concentrate on boats. Harbour scenes — that sort of thing.'

'You've come to the right place, Sammy. Porthcove has a fine old Cornish harbour and fishing boats still work from here.' Keith Parry paused. 'That's it then. Val runs a small shop in the hall where you can buy paints, brushes and paper if you run out.'

'I bet she does,' Bullard said. 'Anything to get more money out of us.'

Parry continued as if he had not been interrupted.

'Breakfast at eight. We'll meet at nine-fifteen and walk down to the harbour together. There's one more to join our group — Wilfred. I've met him before, and he uses pastel. He's staying at the Harbour Inn with his wife.'

'Bit of a snob, is he?' Bullard jeered.

'I'll be giving a demonstration one evening this week,' Keith Parry said. 'And, George, it would help if you could say nice things sometimes.'

'Not nearly so interesting though,' George Bullard said, and laughed.

Linda Snow was up early next morning. She left Duke, her boyfriend, in bed, lit a cigarette and went through to the hall. The front door was open and she heard voices outside.

On the lawn, Jim Fletcher was demonstrating boomerang throwing to Margo and Sammy.

Linda's eyes sparkled with excitement. 'Can I have a go?'

Fletcher smiled. 'Too right you can, Linda.'

She dropped her half-smoked cigarette and trod it carefully into the grass.

The Australian showed her how to grip the curved wooden missile and positioned her, one foot in front of the other, turning her to take advantage of the early morning breeze.

'When you throw, use the wrist. Like this.' He demonstrated with a flick of his wrist. 'Remember, it's all in the wrist action.'

Linda gripped the boomerang at one end, took three or four quick steps forward and flicked it. A breeze caught the crescent of smooth wood and lifted it. It sailed up into the sky and began to curve back towards her.

'Don't take your eye off it,' Fletcher

called. 'Don't try to catch it — get ready to duck.'

Linda watched the boomerang coming back and turned to watch its flight. She was poised ready to duck, but it brought up short and dropped at her feet.

'Good on yer!' Fletcher exclaimed. 'The sheila's got the knack first go.'

'This is a nice idea,' Keith Parry said as he joined them on the lawn. 'I can see you people are getting on well together.'

'Throw again, Linda, while you've got the knack of it.'

She flicked her wrist and the boomerang sailed up and away and began its return flight. Then she noticed George Bullard coming out of the house, a stout figure with a neat dark beard. He bustled over the grass towards them, his eyes gleaming.

'What's this then? A new toy for the kiddies? Haven't you lot grown up yet?'

Jim Fletcher looked at him and looked away. He bent over to retrieve the boomerang, calculated a trajectory and flicked it into the air. The swiftly rotating wood swooped and rose on a current of air. Travelling fast, it came hurtling back.

Fletcher stepped neatly aside and it passed him by.

Bullard saw the approaching boomerang only at the last moment. He tried to step back in a hurry, tripped and fell flat on his face. The missile passed over his prone body.

When he got up, his face was red. He wiped dew from his clothes with a handkerchief. 'You lunatic! You — you dangerous idiot!'

Sammy laughed as Bullard stalked away. Parry frowned and glanced at his watch. 'Almost time for breakfast,' he said.

Fletcher was smiling as he collected his boomerang. They all walked with him to his hatchback, and Margo said with satisfaction, 'That's made my day, that has.'

Fletcher unlocked his car and tossed the boomerang onto the back seat.

'What are those?' Linda asked, pointing at two wooden sticks.

'Those are the real thing,' Fletcher said. 'What you sailed this morning are toys — George was right about that, at least.'

He picked up one of the sticks to show them. It was over a metre in length and looked like the branch of a tree with the bark removed and worn smooth by handling. There was a slight curve to it that was not as pronounced as the curve in a boomerang. The wood was hard and the stick heavy.

'These are what the abos use to hunt with — killing sticks.'

'Do they return too?' Linda asked.

Fletcher shook his head. 'They're not meant to. When one of these hits a 'roo, that animal is meat. A killing stick has a different action from a boomerang. It doesn't go through the air, but end over end along the ground.'

Casually, Fletcher tossed the stick into the back of his car.

Keith Parry said, 'I hope you keep your car locked, Jim. Those things look lethal to me.'

Fletcher seemed mildly irritated. 'I've just explained — they are. And I'm not stupid, you know.'

He locked the car and they went in to breakfast.

2

My Favourite Corpse!

After breakfast, Linda carried her sketching gear around the side of the house to the car park. 'Duke' Dickson was checking the oil and tyres of his Kawasaki 750.

'Oh, there you are, Duke. I'm just off. I've remembered where I saw Jim — it was on television.' Linda sounded excited. 'I knew I'd seen him somewhere before. He was talking about koala bears.'

'Yeah? He gets around, that Aussie. Nice bloke though — not like George.' Duke spat on the tarmac. 'I'll murder that arrogant pig before we leave. I can just see it happening.'

Linda laughed. 'I don't let George worry me because I can see through him. He enjoys needling people. He does it deliberately. You shouldn't let him upset you.'

Duke grunted.

Sammy, strolling around the corner, murmured, 'Easier said than done.' He stood admiring Duke's motorcycle. 'I used to ride a Triumph when I was young — getting too old for that now.'

'Don't you believe it,' Duke said. 'You're never too old to ride — have a nice day, Linda.'

Linda and Sammy set off down the hill towards the harbour, following the rest of the sketching party. Keith Parry and Bullard were leading. Margo and Jim Fletcher dropped back.

'Keith's got lumbered,' Margo said, and made a face. 'I like men, but George is one I can do without.'

Where the hill curved towards the sea, set back from the road, a cottage advertised: *Cornish Cream Teas, Strawberries*.

'I'll be calling in there,' Linda said.

Margo sighed. 'I suppose I will, too, even though I shouldn't. I just love cream but it's no good for my figure.'

Sammy beamed at her. 'Your figure's fine,' he said gallantly.

15

The hill dropped away steeply and tarmac gave way to cobblestones as they entered the village. It was small, consisting of a few fishermen's cottages with pink walls and blue window frames grouped about the harbour. The road joined the quayside, and there was a church on one corner and the inn opposite.

Parry and Bullard waited outside the inn. As the others arrived, a man and woman came out together. The man was dapper and his casual clothes expensively tailored. He carried a folding easel and a large box of pastels.

''Morning, Wilfred,' Parry said briskly. 'Nice to see you again. Good morning, Mrs. Keller.'

Wilfred Keller's wife was large and heavily built. Her homely face was adorned by a faint moustache and her town clothes out of place in a fishing village.

George Bullard stared at Wilfred, then at his wife, and whistled.

'Well, well, what have we here? A lap dog? Wilfred — a real pip-squeak of a name. And you madam — is this the best you could buy in the way of a man?'

Mrs. Keller glared at him, her face gradually turning scarlet. She gave a snort, turned on high heels and retreated inside the inn.

Bullard laughed.

Wilfred Keller regarded him with distaste. 'I'd be careful if I were you,' he said mildly. 'Hilda doesn't appreciate that kind of remark.'

Bullard winked. 'Wealthy, is she? Just the job, Wilf, old boy. Why work when you can live off some old bag, is what I say. Good luck to you.'

'Cut it out, George,' Keith Parry said sharply. 'All right, spread out and begin sketching. I'll work my way around to each of you in time.'

★   ★   ★

At lunchtime they drifted, like iron filings to a magnet, back to the Harbour Inn. Val Courtney had provided sandwiches and they took glasses of beer to the seats outside. A striped awning gave shade from the sun.

17

Margo fanned herself with a sketchpad. 'Another scorcher!'

'It's a real heat-wave, this summer,' Sammy agreed.

Jim Fletcher had brought two large glasses out with him. He downed one and wiped his mouth with the back of his hand.

'It's warm,' he admitted. 'But for real heat you have to go to the desert in Western Australia. Reckon that's why Aussies drink so much beer — that and the short drinking hours.'

'What's it like down under?' Linda asked. 'Duke had the idea of emigrating at one time.'

Fletcher considered for a moment. 'Duke would do all right, I reckon. Things are looser there, more easy-going — know what I mean? A feller who can adapt can survive anywhere.

'Take me, now — I've done a bit of everything in my time. Radio DJ. Pilot with the Flying Doctor Service. Driven a beer truck across the desert — I can tell you, we like our beer.'

He proved his words by half-emptying his second glass.

''Course you can get stuck in a dry river bed — just let your tyres down and inflate 'em the other side. Yeah, I've worked as a stockman and uranium miner. Didn't fancy that for long — too risky with all that radiation stuff floating around. You name it, and I've done it, you bet.'

They were fascinated by Jim Fletcher's reminiscences — all except George Bullard.

He sneered. 'It must be the black blood in you. I expect your grandfather slept with an aborigine.'

'I expect he did,' Fletcher said. 'But these days, the abos have another problem. Their kids sniff petrol, and that can be deadly.'

He drained his glass and began to sing in an exaggerated accent:

'We three Kings of Bankstown Square
We sell ladies' underwear
So fantastic
No elastic
Only a dollar a pair . . . '

Bullard picked up his easel and paint-box. 'I'm not stopping here to listen to a drunken slob.'

'It's time you were all back at work,' Keith Parry said.

Margo Nicholas toiled slowly up the hill on the way to the studio with Sammy. Her sketching bag felt heavier than it had on the way down that morning.

'Let's stop at the tea-rooms for a cuppa,' Sammy suggested.

'I think we'd better,' she said. 'I hadn't realized Cornwall was like this. It's going to kill me if we have to walk up this hill every day.'

'There is a bus,' Sammy said. 'I'll find out what time it runs.'

'Sounds like a good idea.' Margo wondered if he was getting interested in her. She quite liked the little jew and her stars indicated a new romance.

They reached the cottage in the bend of the road and took an outside table, dropping their gear beside their chairs.

'Nice view of the harbour from here,' Sammy said.

Margo kicked off her sandals and wiggled her toes. 'Am I glad to rest my feet?' She lit a cigarette, inhaled, and sighed. 'My clothes are sticking to me.

The first thing I do when we get back is take a bath.'

The waitress arrived and Sammy said, 'Two strawberry teas, with extra cream.'

'I shouldn't really.' Margo protested.

'Nonsense. All this walking will keep you in trim. Anyway, I prefer a woman with something to get hold of.'

Sammy propped his small canvas against a spare chair and looked glumly at it. 'Not exactly an old master.'

Margo said loyally, 'It's not that bad. After all, this is our first day, and you'll improve with practice. I must say, Keith is very helpful.'

'He's all right. How did you get on?'

Margo flipped open her sketchbook as their tea arrived.

'That's great,' Sammy enthused. 'Wish I had your talent.'

'We each do what we can.' Margo helped herself liberally to cream and popped a strawberry into her mouth.

'I like boats,' Sammy said. 'Only I can't draw very well. And this is a good place for boats . . . there's only one fly in the ointment.'

'I know what you mean. George.'

A fire blazed up in Sammy's eyes. 'A ruddy jew baiter! And an artist — I'd never have believed it.'

Margo helped herself to more cream. 'Forget him. These strawberries are lovely, Sammy — eat up. I'm psychic, and I've a feeling about George. No good will come to him, I'm sure.'

George Bullard stood outside the front porch at Porthcove Studios just before dinner and watched young Linda walk across the lawn towards him. He had been studying a flowering shrub and deciding in his mind how he would paint it.

Linda Snow wore tight-fitting jeans and a tee-shirt and her walk had a sensuous hip-swinging style. Duke didn't know what he had there, Bullard thought; it took a mature man to appreciate this girl.

'Hi, beautiful,' he said as she approached. 'How about posing in the nude? You'd make a great model and this outdoor sketching isn't really me.'

She stared blankly at him. 'Pardon?'

'We'll make up a kitty to pay you

something. I'm sure all the men would chip in.'

Linda tossed her blonde hair. 'Get lost!'

A hand gripped him from behind and swung him around. Bullard saw Duke Dickson, his face contorted in fury.

'Keep your hands off my girlfriend, or I'll kill you!'

'You, and whose army?'

Duke balled his hand into a fist and slammed it into Bullard's stomach. As he doubled over in pain, Duke's arm lifted to strike again. But before the blow could land, someone gripped his arm.

'Cool it,' Keith Parry said.

'Yeah, cool it,' Linda echoed. 'I can look after myself.'

'You know I don't like you playing around with other blokes, Linda.' Duke allowed himself to relax, then shrugged. 'Okay, but if George takes one more step out of line, I'll flatten him.'

Parry released Duke and helped Bullard upright. 'You really should think before you open your mouth, George.'

Duke stared thoughtfully at Parry as the tutor helped Bullard into the house.

'That Mr. Keith now, he looks a bit of a poof, but he's got a grip all right. Of course, he took me by surprise.'

'Of course,' Linda said sarcastically. 'Now can we drop this macho stuff?'

Sammy Jacobi and Fletcher were watching, with quiet amusement, as Margo read the tarot cards on the writing table in the common room. She was telling Linda's fortune.

'I see trouble in your life. It will come quite soon — but it will pass, and I see unity with your beloved.'

After dinner, Parry had suggested they relax for an evening. This, after all, was a holiday and not intended to be all work.

The armchairs were deep and comfortable, there was a selection of light reading in the bookcase and a film showing on the television.

George Bullard strolled in.

'The gypsy's warning,' he said contemptuously. 'That old con game — I didn't think anyone fell for that line any more. Crystal balls, seances and table-turning. Nothing but a bag of tricks — talk about getting money under false pretences.'

'No money is involved,' Sammy said. 'Linda asked Margo to read the cards for her.'

'That's right,' Linda said. 'It's only a game really. Everyone reads what the stars foretell in the newspapers, don't they?'

'I don't,' Bullard sneered.

'Perhaps you should,' Margo said quietly. 'Perhaps it might change your attitude if you knew what was in store for you.'

'Rubbish!' Bullard sniffed the air. 'My God, woman, do you bathe in that cheap scent? Try soap and water.'

'Excuse me, Linda.'

Margo Nicholas leaned forward, brass bangles jangling, and seized Bullard's wrist. She stared intently into his palm and spoke in a mystic tone.

'I see . . . I see a deal of unpleasantness. First it moves out from you . . . a dark cloud obscuring your lifeline. Then it returns, like a boomerang.'

Bullard jerked his hand away from her as if scalded. He scowled, and blustered, 'A lot of rubbish.'

He opened the hall door and paused in the doorway. 'Jim, I'm going down to the inn for a drink. Care to join me?'

Fletcher said solemnly, 'Sorry mate, but you know I don't drink.'

Bullard went out, slamming the door, and Linda giggled.

'Damn,' Fletcher said. 'I intended to go out for a drink later. I don't suppose there's another pub within miles.'

Margo looked at Linda, her expression grave. 'It's nothing to laugh at child. I truly am psychic.'

Sammy said, 'If I made a habit of murdering people, George would be my favourite corpse.'

★   ★   ★

The Harbour Inn was not busy when George Bullard pushed open the door and walked in. The landlord, plump and bespectacled, polished glasses behind a bar lit by ships' lanterns. A few locals played dominoes under hanging fishnets decorated with blue-green glass floats.

In a corner seat, Wilfred Keller and his

wife sat having a quiet drink.

'That dreadful man is here,' Hilda said in a carrying voice.

Bullard smiled as he headed straight for them.

'Saw your sketch today, Wilf, old boy.' There was condescension in his voice. 'Not bad, not bad at all. If you want my advice — ' Hilda Keller rose to her feet and said loudly, 'My husband does not require instruction from you. He is a great artist.'

'Not that great,' Bullard said. 'Not as good as me, in fact.'

'Come, Wilfred.'

Hilda swept majestically past Bullard, hand on her husband's arm, steering him towards the staircase leading up to their private room.

Bullard watched them go, laughing, then called out, 'Goodnight, horse-face — goodnight, lap-dog!'

He strolled to the bar.

'Whisky, landlord, a double. No watering it now, and no short-changing me.'

'I shouldn't keep my customers if I did that, sir.'

Bullard stood at the bar counter, sipping his drink. A few feet away, a man wearing a blue jersey that smelled of fish watched him steadily.

The man moved closer and asked in accented English; 'You are, perhaps, a painter, m'sieur?'

'I am a painter,' Bullard agreed. 'And you're a damned Frog!'

He swallowed his whisky and walked towards the door.

The French fisherman stared after him.

3

Miss Eaton Agrees

Wilfred and Hilda Keller were taking lunch in the dining room of the Harbour Inn. The tablecloth was white and starched, the glasses sparkled in a beam of sunlight, and the cutlery gleamed.

When the door opened. Hilda said, 'Oh, dear — one of your party has just come in.'

Wilfred glanced around. 'It's not George. Jim's all right.'

Fletcher crossed to them, smiling easily. 'G'day, mate. Nice to meet you, Mrs. Keller. Thought I'd have a change from sandwiches today — d'you mind if I join you?'

'Take a seat,' Wilfred invited.

'What's on the menu?'

'We're having the fish,' Mrs. Keller said. 'It's caught locally, and I always think it makes such a difference to the flavour when it's fresh.'

As the waitress appeared, Fletcher ordered. 'I'll take fish — and a pint of lager to go with it.' He turned to Wilfred and made a face. 'I got stuck with George — that bloke gives me the needle.'

'An oaf,' Hilda remarked.

'Not a pleasant type,' Wilfred said absently, glancing through his sketch-book.

'D'you mind if I take a look?'

'Of course not, Jim.'

Fletcher turned the pages slowly, studying each charcoal sketch in turn.

'Yeah, you've got something all right. I was admiring your pastel of a rock formation yesterday, and I said to myself, that bloke's got it.'

'He's very good,' Hilda purred, while Fletcher paused at a black-and-line study of some fishermen's cottages. 'Nice, very nice. 'D'you sell much of your work. Wilfred? Ever had a West End showing?'

'Only when my wife's paid for it.'

'I was happy to do that,' she said quickly.

Fletcher drank his lager as the fish

arrived. 'What you need is an agent. Someone to push your work — make a name. After that, it's easy.'

Hilda Keller paused over her food. 'You seem to know something about it, Mr. — ?'

'Fletcher's the name. Yeah, I suppose I do — there's no point in false modesty. I've been at it a few years, talking on radio, demonstrating on telly, all around the world. Say, I might be able to fix something for Wilfred. Give him a hand, like . . . '

* * *

In the kitchen at Porthcove Studios, Joyce Willis, the cook, flushed with anger as she prepared dinner with Val's assistance.

'That Bullard person's never satisfied, is he? No matter what the menu says, he wants steak when we serve fish, and curry when lamb's on. I don't know why you let him get away with it, Mrs. Courtney, I really don't. He's a pain in the neck.'

Joyce slammed down a saucepan on the stainless steel table.

'Yes, well,' Val said mildly. 'I might agree with you — in private — but he is paying, you know. And we do try to give satisfaction.'

Joyce sniffed expressively.

'Satisfaction, is it? That one? Never! No matter what you put in front of him, he'll want something different. No matter what I cook special for him, he'll complain. You ought to send him packing, that's what. I hear things, you know — he's upsetting everybody.'

She chopped onions rapidly with a sharp knife.

'Mind your fingers,' Val said. 'Just try to stay calm.' She sighed, and wished she could send George Bullard packing.

George Bullard moved quietly along the passage in the annexe towards the room that Linda shared with Duke Dickson. Lucky man, he thought enviously; too young to know what he'd got there, too young to appreciate her.

He'd seen her arrive back from the harbour and heard her splashing about in the bathroom, but he wasn't sure if Duke was in their room or not. Nothing ventured, nothing seen, he told himself.

He paused with his ear against the door. He heard small movements but no voices. He turned the handle and opened the door without knocking.

Linda lay on the bed wearing a pair of bikini pants and smoking a cigarette. When she saw him, she put out her tongue.

'That's rude,' he said.

A voice came from behind the door. 'Seen all you want, you dirty old man?'

Bullard flushed. 'I just came to see — '

'I know what you came to see,' Duke said contemptuously. 'You can look, and that's all you can do. Now beat it.'

He gave Bullard the finger.

As Bullard closed the door and went back to his own room, he heard Linda laughing.

The air was still warm and scented with blossom. The sky was cloudless. Margo and Sammy strolled side by side in the grounds of the studio after dinner.

'I'm beginning to wish I'd never come,' Sammy said gloomily. 'George never lets up, does he?'

Margo made a rude noise.

'Ignore him, Sammy. If you let him see he's getting you down, he won't stop. Ignore him and he'll get tired of baiting you and go away.'

'I wish he would. Permanently.'

They walked slowly in a companionable silence, then Margo said. 'It's not only George. It's this heat wave — we're just not used to this kind of weather. Everyone's on edge.'

They circled the goldfish pond set in the lawn and admired the roses. Margo was looking thoughtful.

'Penny for them,' Sammy said.

'Do you sometimes wonder about Jim?'

'The Aussie? He seems all right.'

'I wonder about him. He tells a good story, but doesn't he lay it on a bit too thick? I wonder if he's really been outback.'

'It's a thought,' Sammy agreed. 'But does it matter? Where's the harm?'

Val Courtney relaxed in a comfortable chair in the private sitting room upstairs. She sipped at a glass of white wine and Mozart played softly in the background. Her husband, Reggie, sat opposite, cupping a tumbler of whisky.

It was what they called the quiet hour, before going to bed, when they could forget the day's cares and unwind. But not tonight.

Keith Parry paced restlessly up and down the carpet between them, waving his arms dramatically.

'I'm fed up with Bullard, I tell you. He's upsetting the students and ruining my course.' His voice rose shrilly. 'The only time I can get any teaching done is when he's not around. When he's there, he destroys the friendly feeling I try to build up with the party.'

Reggie sipped his whisky. 'A nasty piece of work, all right. Luckily I don't have much to do with him, but I've heard him a couple of times.'

Parry shuddered.

'I get him all the time. He's a menace, and I'm not sure I can take much more. He poisons the atmosphere.'

'Oh, I expect you'll manage, Keith. You usually do.' Val forced a smile. 'You've had difficult students before.'

'Difficult, yes. But no-one like Bullard — he's impossible. I swear he enjoys making trouble. I'm convinced he came here only to cause trouble.'

'That's going a bit far, isn't it?' Reggie protested. 'I mean, he wouldn't know anyone before he arrived, would he?'

Parry stopped pacing to brood. 'He might. I don't know. I thank my lucky stars I've never encountered him before. He's a sadist — I've never had such an unhappy week.'

Val said, 'He's managed to upset Joyce as well. If she leaves, we're really in trouble.'

Parry began to pace up and down again, then turned to face her. The Mozart recording came to an end and his high-pitched voice sounded twice as loud in the silence.

'You're the brains of this outfit, Val. It's up to you. You've got to do something to stop him, or this studio is finished!'

★   ★   ★

Miss Isabel Eaton sat in a swivel chair with her feet on the desk and contemplated her legs below the hem of a brightly coloured dirndl skirt. They reminded her of a pair of hockey sticks.

She poured liquid from a square bottle labelled Kentucky Bourbon Whiskey into a tumbler and sipped. The label was genuine.

At her back, the window was wide open and the dust and heated air and traffic noises of Grays Inn Road came in. Her small office on the third floor smelt of stale cigarette smoke, and the building cleaners had firm instructions not to disturb the layer of dust on a rusting green filing cabinet.

A cigarette burnt itself out in a metal ashtray. Miss Eaton didn't much care for smoking but it helped the image she was trying to build up. There was a cigarette burn on the desk and the metal waste bin, ex-army supplies like the filing cabinet, overflowed with junk mail. Everything about the shabby office was a pose.

She picked up a much-thumbed copy of *Death Wears Red Garters*, a favourite Sam Pike novel, and read:

A man came through the door with a gun in his hand. It was a big .45 automatic. There was a streak of red flame and a slug blasted over my head.

Suddenly there was the smell of fear in the room, like sludge from a sewer.

I dived across the blonde on the bed — she was a genuine blonde, I noticed in passing — and slammed into the mobster. He bounced off the wall and slumped to the floor . . .

The obligatory blonde; the real life of a private eye was never like that, Miss Eaton reflected sadly. She never ended up in bed with a hunk of man, nor had she ever been slugged in a dark alley or fired a shot in anger.

The telephone rang and she put on her tough American voice to answer.

'Eaton Investigations.'

'Belle? It's Val Courtney. Val, from St. Agatha's — the name was Forbes then. Remember?'

Middle-age dropped away from Miss Eaton along with her tough accent. St. Agatha's College for Young Ladies, gym tunics and the class bell, hockey and sausage-rolls in the dorm after lights out . . .

'Of course I remember, Val! How are

you? Are you in London?'

'I'm harassed, and speaking from Porthcove in Cornwall, along the coast from Penzance. My husband, Reg, and I have a studio here, and we need advice. I read somewhere that you're running a private detective agency and thought you might know the answer.'

'Glad to help an old girl.'

'We've got a problem student — George Bullard by name — a most obnoxious person who upsets everyone. I've asked him to leave and he simply laughed at me, and I'm at my wit's end.'

'I'll soon get rid of him for you,' Miss Eaton said.

She had a vision of getting out of London in a heat wave to a cool breeze off the sea.

'Oh, I do hope you can.'

Miss Eaton said, 'Nothing to it. I'll run down and sort out this Bullard for you.'

*   *   *

'You what?'

Reggie Courtney looked at his wife in

39

astonishment. His voice was unusually sharp.

'A detective? Coming here? Why on earth did you do that?'

They had met at the bottom of the staircase in the hall. Val coming down to go to the kitchen, Reggie coming in from the garden and going upstairs to wash.

'You heard what Keith said. He wanted me to do something about Bullard.'

'That's true. But he didn't mean you to call in the police. You know Keith — he's artistic, he dramatizes. One awkward student won't ruin us.'

'Well, Bullard refused to leave. And Belle isn't police — she's a private investigator.'

Reggie relaxed but still looked doubtful. 'She might upset the students, all the same. Nobody likes a snooper. Don't forget they're our bread and butter.'

'I'm sure they'll be as pleased to see the last of Bullard as I'll be.'

'I don't doubt that, but — '

'I was at school with Belle. She was always reading those dreadful American stories about private eyes and finding out things for us. I'm sure she's very good, and won't upset anyone.'

Reggie Courtney sighed. 'And she's coming?'

'Yes. You'll see, she'll know how to handle George Bullard.'

4

Wilfred Goes Missing

When Miss Eaton arrived at the converted mews off Chelsea Reach she had made her home, she began to pack a suitcase.

Sherry, a large blue Persian cat, prowled around her restlessly. Sherry knew her mistress was going away, and protested loudly.

'Stop it, Sherry. You're coming too.'

Miss Eaton opened a bottle of dry sherry and poured a little into a saucer. The Persian purred and rubbed silky fur against her legs; she was one cat who liked her tipple. She lapped delicately until the saucer was clean and curled up in her basket to sleep it off.

Miss Eaton's home, unlike her office, was spotless. Behind glass in a row of bookcases reposed her personal library of *Sam Pike* novels, and an almost complete collection of *Black Mask* detective magazines.

She packed a tracksuit and swimming costume, her Smith and Wesson and binoculars. She showered and inspected her slight figure in the mirror; fit at forty, and her sharply pointed nose might be taken as an indication of her chosen profession.

She dressed for comfort and carried the cat basket, with Sherry still asleep, out to her car. She returned, to get her case and an early *Sam Pike* novel, *Model For Murder*, and locked up.

As she drove out of London, Sherry dreamed of fat mice in a cat Heaven in the back of the small Fiat saloon. Miss Eaton drove along the M3 motorway into the west country through the early evening. She felt relaxed and drove at an unhurried pace

She stopped at a motel outside Exeter and booked a room for one night. There was no hurry. She regarded this job as a bit of a holiday, a chance to gossip about old times with Val. Bullard would be no problem.

As she dropped off to sleep, with Sherry on the bed at her feet, Miss Eaton wondered idly what was happening at Porthcove.

★ ★ ★

George Bullard chuckled to himself as he wiped his brushes. He was alone in the grounds of Porthcove Studios. His easel was set up in the shade, and trees screened him from any casual eye.

He was reasonably pleased with the result he had captured in oils: the bloom of dark red roses against the pale yellow of sunlit grass.

Pleased, too, with the way he had stirred things up during the last few days. It always amazed him how easy it was to upset people.

He looked towards the house. Parry and the rest of the holiday painters were down at the harbour. Courtney had gone too. Fish again for dinner, he thought; I'll have a moan about that. Val was shopping in Penzance.

The only sound was a drone of bees

over the flowerbeds on a sleepy afternoon. There was no traffic about. The part-time gardener was in the greenhouse at the rear of the studio. The cook, he'd learnt, invariably took an afternoon nap.

'A chance to take a quick look around,' he thought, and walked around the pond towards the front porch. He whistled an old-fashioned tune under his breath.

'Never know what I might find . . . '

* * *

Hilda Keller sat beneath a sunshade at a table outside the tearooms between the inn and the studio. The afternoon was hot and she ate strawberries with cream as she studied the view through binoculars.

They were, of course, essential for bird watching — and useful for keeping an eye on Wilfred. Where, she wondered, was her husband at this moment?

The tearoom, halfway up the hill, was an ideal spot for observing the coastline. There was a clear view of the harbour and pink-and-blue cottages below.

She could see some of the painters at

work and watched their tutor move briskly from one to another. The blonde girl was alone near the rocks that jutted out from the headland. The jew had set up his easel on the quay close to the fishing boats. There was no sign of Wilfred.

She focused on a chough, a crow-like bird with a red bill, as it wheeled above the cliffs.

She turned in her chair and looked up at the studio. She could see only the roof of the building, and the upper row of windows. There was somebody at one of the windows. Staff, she imagined. She'd heard that the top floor was private and off-limits to students, so it couldn't be Wilfred.

Hilda sighed and put her binoculars away. She got to her feet and began a slow descent to the village.

She couldn't hurry; she was too heavily built for that — and no beauty. She knew Wilfred had married her for her money and didn't care. He was her husband; she loved him and intended to keep him.

She reached the cottages and moved

along the quay, lips pursed and handbag swinging. Sammy was painting a group of boats in the harbour. She didn't like talking to a jew, but he might know something.

'Have you seen my husband?'

At least Jacobi was polite. 'Not since lunch. We split up, you know, and find our own subjects.'

Hilda walked on, beyond the harbour, to where Keith Parry was demonstrating the use of water colour to Linda.

'Keep your washes broad. Sketch in the subject lightly — ignore finicky detail.'

She felt a sense of relief that, at least, Wilfred wasn't chasing this girl. Sometimes she imagined he had a roving eye.

'Have you seen Wilfred?'

Parry glanced up from the sketch.

'Not yet, Mrs. Keller. It takes time to get around to everyone. Do you have any idea of the subject he was going for this afternoon?'

Hilda shook her head and turned back to where the gypsy-looking woman was drawing a view of some cottages.

Wilfred wasn't with her and she hadn't

seen him since lunchtime.

She couldn't see that nice Australian, either. Perhaps he and Wilfred were together.

Hilda kept looking.

★   ★   ★

After dinner, they met in the studio. Keith Parry had arranged a large sketchpad on an easel, and held a handful of brushes. He had paints already squeezed onto a palette.

The group sat on stools in a semi-circle about him.

'Everyone comfortable? Good. I shan't spend long over this demonstration, just long enough to give you a few ideas, I hope. I've noticed during the last few days that some of you are stuck doing the same kind of thing over and over again. And it really is a good idea to experiment a bit.

'For this demo, I'm using acrylic paints. These are quick drying, and useful for outdoor work. So, a few sketches in different styles which you can try for yourselves later. It can help you get out of the rut, like this . . . '

He propped a colour print of Porthcove harbour on a second easel.

'This is something I did a few years ago. Now, as Cézanne might have seen it.'

Parry sketched in a few cubes and cylinders in warm and cool tones, tore off the sheet and began again.

'This time, Van Gogh.'

The harbour re-appeared, now constructed of vigorous swirling brushstrokes

'Or Paul Klee.'

Another sheet, an abstract with lines like hieroglyphs.

'Matisse.'

The harbour appeared as a design in one plane with pure colours and arabesque lines.

Parry washed out his brushes.

'Do you see? It's the same scene all the time — but looked at in a different way. Tomorrow, I'd like each of you to look at your subject with a fresh eye. Experiment. If you tackle an old theme in a new way, I'm sure you'll find it exciting. And you'll go back with some fresh ideas to develop at home.'

Parry looked at his class. Linda appeared doubtful. Margo was flushed.

'Nothing to say, George?'

For once, George Bullard kept quiet. He looked thoughtfully from the different sketches, to Keith Parry, and smiled.

It was not a nice smile.

★　★　★

Linda heard Duke's bike revving up and hurried through the common room to the hall carrying a crash helmet. Val Courtney was locking the door of the art shop, and Linda said:

'We're having an evening out. Duke says there's a roadhouse on the way to Penzance, so we're going for a drink and dance.'

'That's fine,' Val said, smiling. 'It's your holiday — enjoy yourselves.'

Duke Dickson appeared in the doorway in black leathers.

'Yeah, I've been exploring while Linda was painting. We might be late back, okay?'

'Of course. We don't lock the front

door — there's no need to around here. Just don't make too much noise as you come in. Remember, other people are sleeping. And turn off the lights, please.'

'You bet,' Duke said, and grinned. 'We'll be like a couple of mice.'

★ ★ ★

Bullard watched Duke and Linda leave on the Kawasaki, and Val Courtney go upstairs. Fletcher had gone down to the inn. Parry was still cleaning up in the studio, and Sammy and Margo were in the common room; the door was shut but he could hear their voices.

He waited in the hall, jingling coins in his pocket.

When Parry came out of the studio, Bullard stopped him.

'I'd like to have a chat with you sometime. In private.'

'Yes, all right.' The tutor forced a smile. 'Any time. That's what I'm here for — to help with any problems you have.'

George Bullard smiled.

'Oh, it's not my problem,' he said

51

lightly. 'Shall we say, in an hour's time? It's a pleasant evening. We might even take a gentle stroll while we chat . . . '

★   ★   ★

Miss Eaton drove towards Porthcove.

After leaving Exeter, she took the A30 to Penzance, and then a local road that resembled a switchback. It dropped into a series of small bays and then climbed steeply up again. The road was narrow and bordered by grey stone walls.

The morning sky remained clear and bright with sunlight and there was little traffic, except for a tractor that delayed her until it turned into a field.

A farmer's dog ran alongside the Fiat, barking furiously until Sherry sat up and spat at it. This really was a delightful piece of rural England, Miss Eaton thought with approval.

Presently she came to a sign that read: *Porthcove*.

Studios. She slowed to turn into the driveway, and was forced to use her brakes.

There was a chain across the entrance and a uniformed constable standing beside it.

'Sorry, miss,' the constable said, 'but you can't come in here.'

Miss Eaton put on her Sam Pike voice. 'Is that so? Waal, let me tell you I'm expected by Mrs. Courtney.'

'The Inspector's orders, miss. No-one in, no-one out.'

'Inspector? Say, what's going on here?'

'This,' the constable said officiously, 'is the murder scene. An artist named Bullard has got himself killed.'

5

The Body on the Lawn

Val Courtney came running across the lawn towards them.

Miss Eaton was mildly surprised, even though some years had passed. At school, Val had been a gangling young girl; she had filled out now and her bones were well-fleshed. She wore a smart business suit.

She arrived out of breath. 'Belle?'

'Yes. It appears that your little problem has been solved.'

Val shivered. 'Don't say that . . . we'll be ruined.'

'Oh, I shouldn't think so. There's nothing like a nice juicy murder to bring in the cash customers.'

Val turned to the uniformed officer and her voice was firm, almost bossy. 'Let her through please, constable — she's an old friend, staying with me.'

The constable unfastened the chain and Miss Eaton drove her Fiat through and parked at the side of the house. She switched off the engine and got out, leaving Sherry in the car.

'I'm so glad you're here,' Val said. 'I simply don't know what I'm doing or how I'm going to cope. Reggie — my husband — is worried to death. Bullard upset everyone! He deserved to die — a most unpleasant person — but why did it have to happen here?' Her voice ended on a wailing note.

Miss Eaton looked across the lawn to a group in front of the house. An area had been roped off. She saw two police detectives conversing behind a low canvas wall.

Val noticed her gaze, and grimaced. 'I suppose you'll want to see . . . professional curiosity. I can't face it.'

But she walked with Miss Eaton towards the scene of the crime.

As Miss Eaton approached, the doctor rose from beside the body sprawled on the grass. Uniformed men were searching among the shrubbery.

The body lay half-hidden by shrubs, away from the path leading from the car park to the front door of the house. It lay face down and she saw dried blood on the back of the head. In life he had been stout with a neat beard; in death, he seemed to have shrunk and appeared small and insignificant.

A stick, looking like the bent branch of a tree with the bark removed, lay beside the body of George Bullard.

The doctor said, 'I don't have any real doubt, Inspector. The victim was struck down from behind, and his murderer left the weapon here. Curious sort of thing — polished by handling, I'd say.'

The Inspector was big and beefy, his hair streaked with grey. His blue serge suit was shiny with wear.

He asked, 'How long since he was killed?'

'Last night, early morning. Roughly, about midnight.'

'Well, I'd better start seeing people.' He addressed the other detective: 'Constable, make sure the weapon goes to the lab, though I doubt there'll be any prints.'

'Aye, sir.' The detective-constable was a young man, a head taller, with a fresh face and ginger hair.

The Inspector looked around and saw Val.

'Mrs. Courtney, I'll need a room where I can interview people. And a list of residents, staff and — er — artists.'

'I'll arrange that, Inspector.'

He stared at Miss Eaton. 'Who are you? How did you get in here?'

Val said quickly, 'I asked Isabel down to deal with Bullard — before he died, of course. He was making trouble and, obviously, I didn't know he . . . this would happen. She's just arrived.'

Miss Eaton opened her handbag to take out a card, and the Inspector pounced on her bag.

'What's this? A gun?' He sounded annoyed. 'Do you have a license to carry that?'

Miss Eaton pulled out her Smith and Wesson. 'Nope. Figured I didn't need one.'

The Inspector regarded her with disbelief. 'You don't know you need a license to carry a hand gun?'

He took the gun from her and studied it closely. 'A replica!'

The constable covered his mouth with his hand.

'It's good for my image,' Miss Eaton said, and handed over a business card:

EATON INVESTIGATIONS
Private And Confidential Enquiries

'A private detective, for God's sake!' The Inspector snorted in disgust. 'Just what I need — first, a bunch of artists, and now a female private eye.'

The constable looked as if he were trying to repress a smile.

'Just stay out of my way. This is a murder enquiry. Get under my feet, and I'll pinch you for obstructing the law.'

'Don't get tough with me,' Miss Eaton said in a hard American voice.

The Inspector stamped off, and Val took her arm.

'You must stay, Belle — overnight, at least. I insist . . . coming all this way, and I need moral support. Reggie isn't a lot of use. I mean — he's handy about the house and garden, but I have to run everything else. And I'm not feeling up to it at the moment.'

'Of course I'll stay,' Miss Eaton said briskly. 'I wouldn't miss this for anything. It's the first time I've been involved with murder.'

She returned to her car to collect her case, and let Sherry out. The Blue Persian stalked in a circle, sniffing the air suspiciously.

'Isn't he a beauty!' Val exclaimed in admiration.

'She,' Miss Eaton corrected.

Sherry crossed the lawn to the pond and stared into the water.

'She's after the goldfish,' Val said.

'Sherry!'

The cat turned at Miss Eaton's call, hesitated, then followed her into the house. There was a pay phone and stairs in the hall, a door with the sign *Art Shop* on the left, and another door on the right.

A small man with a gloomy expression came down the stairs. 'You'll be the detective, I suppose. I reckon we've got enough of them running around already.'

'That's not very polite,' Val said. 'Belle's come to help us. My husband, Reggie.'

'Yes, dear. Sorry — er — Belle. I wasn't thinking.'

A willowy young man moved gracefully along the passage. He wore tailored slacks, an open-necked shirt with a buttercup-yellow scarf about his throat. As he came nearer, Miss Eaton decided he wasn't as young as he looked. He drawled, 'What's the drill, Val? Do we carry on as usual, or what?'

'Keith Parry, our resident tutor,' Val introduced. 'Keith, this is Belle, an old friend of mine.'

Parry showed interest. 'Ah, the private tec — Reggie mentioned you were coming. A pity you didn't arrive a bit earlier — we might have avoided this unpleasantness.'

Sherry rubbed herself against Val's legs and sniffed warily at her husband. As she approached the tutor, her back arched and her tail went up.

Parry sneezed.

'Oh dear . . . and I like cats. I really do.

It's just that I'm allergic to them. Their fur acts like pollen, and sets off my asthma.'

Miss Eaton said politely, 'Some people are like that, unfortunately.'

★ ★ ★

Detective Inspector Reid surveyed the common room that Mrs. Courtney had provided for use as an interview room.

'Right, constable, let's get organized.' He cleared the table by dumping a pile of art magazines onto an armchair. 'I'll have the table here . . . one chair each side. Push the other stuff back out of the way.'

Together, they rearranged the furniture to the Inspector's liking.

'You take a corner seat so you get them in profile. Got your pad and pencil? You take shorthand, I suppose?'

'Yes sir.'

'Right then.'

Reid sat down, facing the door, and gave a brief look around the room. There was a painting of fishing boats entering harbour on the wall.

'The local harbour,' the constable said. 'A nice picture.'

'You're not here as an art critic. Keep your mind on the job.'

Local men, Reid thought, country yokels. Well, he'd show this one how a Scotland Yard man operated. He scanned the list Mrs. Courtney had provided.

'I'll see — who was it found the body? Mrs. Hilda Keller. Her first. Right, wheel her in, constable.'

6

Official Enquiries

Hilda Keller marched into the interview room and sat down facing the Inspector. She grasped a handbag in her ample lap.

'I'm sorry to have kept you waiting, Inspector, but I'm not accustomed to this kind of situation. I am hardly recovered from the shock.'

'That's understandable. Will you give your full name and permanent address to the constable, please?'

Reid waited while Detective Constable Trewin wrote down these particulars. Looking at her, he thought: formidable. West End clothes — if not Paris.

'Now, Mrs. Keller,' he said briskly. 'I'd like you to tell me, in your own words, exactly how you came to find the body. It was early morning, I believe — and I understand you're staying with your husband at the inn in the village.'

'I chose to stay at the inn because I like my comfort. I doubt if the accommodation here is first class. When I awoke this morning, Wilfred — my husband — had gone. That's unusual, so early in the day, so I went looking for him.'

Reid raised an eyebrow. 'And you thought he might have come to the studio?'

'That's what I thought. Yes.'

'And found the body?'

'Yes.' Hilda Keller shuddered. 'It was most upsetting. Of course, at first I thought there had been an accident — someone injured or taken ill. Naturally, I approached to see if I could help.'

'Naturally. And — ?'

'It was obvious, from the blood on the back of his head . . . and when I saw who it was . . . '

'Yes, Mrs. Keller?'

Hilda's smile was not pleasant. 'I stopped worrying, Inspector. I simply thought that dreadful man had got what he deserved. A most unpleasant person.'

'Yes. I gather he was generally disliked. But disliked enough to murder?'

She didn't answer.

Reid pressed home his point. 'Disliked enough to murder?' he repeated. 'Surely that would indicate a special kind of hatred?'

'It would seem so, Inspector. One of the painting group staying here must have done it — that's obvious, I imagine.'

'And then Mr. Jacobi appeared?'

'The jew? Yes. A common man — he came out of the house and asked what had happened.'

'When did you last see George Bullard alive?'

'Oh, let me think. It must have been a couple of days, at least. I avoided him when I could, but he was persistent in his attentions. Most persistent.'

'That'll do for now, Mrs. Keller. I may want to see you later.'

As she left the room, Reid sighed. The local man had probably never had a murder enquiry before and wouldn't be much help.

'Did you get all of that down, constable?'

'Yes sir.'

'Jacobi next.'

When Sammy Jacobi came in and sat down, Reid stared at the swarthy skin and hook nose and wondered. He had a feeling they'd met before.

'I understand you saw Mrs. Keller with the body,' he said abruptly.

'Sort of, Inspector. I just opened the front door, and there she was, bending over him.'

'You were up early then?'

'Earlier than I realized. I knew Jim — Fletcher, that is — was demonstrating boomerang throwing, and I wanted to have another go. But my watch was on the blink so I was too early. Or Jim was late this morning.'

'And what did you think when you saw her?'

Jacobi grinned. 'Thought she'd done him in, what else? It was a sure thing someone would the way he went about needling everyone.'

'Including you, of course.'

'True, but we Jews are used to that sort of thing. I didn't let Bullard worry me — I've heard worse in my time.'

'He was killed with a boomerang — or was it a killing stick?'

'I wouldn't know, Inspector. You'll have to ask our expert that one.'

'I shall. Right. That's all for now.'

Reid waited with some impatience for Trewin to complete his notes. The Cornishman was not the fastest writer of shorthand he'd known . . .

Then he remarked, 'Interesting. Jacobi says he saw her bending over the body — and thought she'd done it.'

'The doctor says she was killed late last night,' Trewin objected.

'And, as a jew, Bullard didn't worry him. I wonder. It could be — perhaps. But I got the impression Jacobi wouldn't worry a lot if suspicion fell on Mrs. Keller, and that does interest me. I'm sure I've seen his face before. I'll have to check him out with the Yard . . . all right, constable, I'll see Fletcher next.'

Jim Fletcher looked unhappy as he walked into the interview room.

'Sit down, Mr. Fletcher,' Reid said blandly. 'You're Australian, I believe? Just give your resident British address to the constable, please. How long have you been in this country?'

'About six months, I reckon.'

'Now, I understand that you've identified the murder weapon as one of your boomerangs — '

'Killing stick,' Fletcher corrected automatically.

'Literally, in this case. I've heard that you've been teaching some of the holiday painters how to throw a boomerang. I'd like you to tell me which of them is good at it.'

'You're on the wrong track, Inspector. It wouldn't make any difference — '

Reid interrupted sharply. 'I'll decide that. Just give me the name — or names.'

Fletcher answered with obvious reluctance. 'Young Linda. It's a knack, see? Some people catch on quick, some don't. She was good from the first go.' Admiration crept into his voice. 'A natural.' He paused, then:

'But, Inspector, I insist you listen to me. A killing stick is quite different. A boomerang is only a plaything — abos hunt with killing sticks, and the throwing technique is quite different. You don't launch one into the air, and it doesn't return. It travels end over end along the ground.'

'I believe you threw a boomerang at Bullard. Isn't that dangerous?'

'Could have been — he saw it coming, and ducked.'

Reid made a small smile. 'And now you're telling me that only you can handle a throwing stick.'

'Probably I am — here. And don't think I don't know that makes me your number one suspect. It's my stick, and I know how to use it, but — '

'But you're going to tell me anyone could have used it as a club, Mr. Fletcher. I accept that. The stick was in your car, and the car was locked.'

'Right on.'

'When did you last see it?'

'Yesterday morning. When I returned the boomerangs we used before breakfast.'

'So it could have been taken any time during the day?'

'I guess so.'

'Who knew about the killing stick?'

'Anyone who was boomerang-throwing early in the mornings. Most of our group, that is. Except Wilfred — and Duke.'

Reid studied the gaunt face beneath close-cropped hair.

'Do you have any enemies, Mr. Fletcher? Is there anyone here who doesn't like you?'

'Not that I know of. We're strangers — just met for the first time.'

'I wonder if that's true?' Reid spoke his thought aloud, almost absently. 'You were up late this morning?'

'Yeah, a boozy night, I'm afraid.'

'Did you see Bullard late last night?'

'No.'

'That's all for the moment. Ask Mrs. Courtney to step in, please.'

Reid thought: might as well see what Trewin makes of it. If he can think, that is.

'Well, what d'you say, constable?'

'Someone deliberately used the stick to throw suspicion on Fletcher?'

'It's one possibility. Why use the killing stick at all? There must be plenty of other weapons around. Could be it was just handy, of course — anyone can break into a car these days.'

'It could cut down the number of suspects, sir.'

'Obviously — '

Valerie Courtney walked in and sat down at the table across from the Inspector. Her face had lost colour. She folded her hands in her lap and sat motionless, obviously striving to remain outwardly calm.

'First of all, Mrs. Courtney, I'd like Bullard's home address and anything you know about him. Anything at all. Has he been here before?'

'Really, Inspector — do you seriously believe I would have allowed him to come a second time?'

'I suppose not,' Reid admitted. 'An awkward customer, I gather.'

Val gave him a wan smile. 'To put it mildly, I'm surprised he wasn't murdered long ago if he carried on like that all the time.'

'That's something we'll be looking into.'

'He gave an address in Birmingham

— I have details in the office — but I know no more about him. We don't go into personal details, although Keith — Parry, our resident tutor — likes us to ask what painting experience the students have. Bullard claimed to have a lot of experience.'

'We'll be investigating his background, of course,' Reid said. 'I suppose it could be an outsider — someone who followed him here. Did he know anyone here before he arrived?'

Val shook her head. 'They're all first time students at Porthcove.'

Reid took his time filling a pipe while he watched her.

'So you asked this private detective — Eaton — to come here. Why? Who first suggested this? What did you think she could do?'

'I phoned Belle because I thought Bullard would get the studio a bad name if he weren't dealt with. He upset the other students, and we can't afford that sort of reputation. When I asked him to leave, he laughed and said it was just a bit of fun — that he'd paid for two weeks and intended to stay the full time.'

'And Miss Eaton? Where does she come in?'

'I felt desperate. Keith said I'd got to do something because Bullard was ruining his class. Reggie isn't much use when it comes to sorting out trouble. I remembered an article I'd read about Belle being a private investigator, and thought she might have come up against a similar situation in her job. So she might know a way of handling it. Of getting rid of him.'

She shuddered.

Reid puffed on his pipe with an appearance of satisfaction. 'I'll see your husband next.'

While they waited, Trewin ventured, 'Could be a motive there. If Bullard was putting students off. The studio's livelihood. I wonder how this place stands financially?'

'That's something else we'll be looking at,' Reid said. Perhaps Trewin was capable of learning after all.

'Parry suggested Mrs. Courtney do something — '

'So perhaps she did.'

When Reggie Courtney came in and sat down, he wore a look of weary resignation.

'I'd like you to tell me whatever you can about George Bullard.'

Courtney pulled a face. 'I didn't have much to do with him, luckily, but I heard things. A nasty piece of work.'

'You're a sort of general handyman here?'

'You've got it in one. Val runs the place really — I don't have a head for business.'

'Is the house locked up at night?'

'Never. These people are on holiday and if they want a late night out, they're entitled to it. Not much crime around here anyway — burglary, I mean.'

'Did you know this Eaton woman was arriving?'

'Val told me after she'd invited her. I was a bit surprised.'

'Did you approve?'

Courtney shrugged. 'It's up to Val. What she says goes, more or less. I stay with the odd jobs and Keith does the tutoring.'

Reid knocked out his pipe.

'All right, I'll see the tutor next. Parry, isn't it? He should be able to tell us something — he was in contact with Bullard every day.'

When the door closed, Trewin said, 'Nothing much there.'

Reid bared his teeth. 'Not unless they're in it together.'

Keith Parry glided into the room like a ballet dancer coming on stage. He tossed back floppy straw-coloured hair and put on a brave smile as he took the seat opposite the Inspector.

'But of course I shall co-operate in every way. This unpleasantness really must come to an end.'

'First off, did you know Bullard from before? Or any of the students?'

Parry lifted his hands in horror. 'Bullard? Never! I'd have resigned first. All these students are new to Porthcove. I suppose — though I doubt it — that anyone of them might have known Bullard before, but the only one — or should I say two? — I knew are the Kellers. She's got money, in case you didn't know, and Wilfred is serious about painting. They move from one course to another through the season. I met Wilfred when I was tutoring in Warwickshire.'

Reid asked, 'Is there anyone you can think of who might have lost his cool with Bullard?'

'Anyone? My dears, everyone!' Parry's hands fluttered like butterflies. 'Such a dreadful person — he was spoiling my class, I tell you. He upset — deliberately, I'm certain — everybody in turn. Including Val. And our cook. A simply awful person. It's a great pity no-one killed him before he arrived here.'

Reid's gaze moved to the painting on the wall. 'One of yours?'

'Yes, indeed. One of my better efforts, I think. If you're interested, the asking price is two hundred.'

'I'm not that interested. Was Bullard any good as a painter?'

'He wasn't bad,' Parry admitted. 'One of the more experienced students. He'd obviously done quite a lot of painting, but he wasn't as good as he thought he was.'

He frowned, and asked: 'What can I do,

Inspector? Can I continue with the class? Take them out sketching?'

Reid looked thoughtfully at the light blue eyes, the blond hair.

'I don't see why not — after my questioning is completed. Of course, no-one must leave here without my permission, and everyone must be prepared to answer further questions, as necessary. But I don't see why you shouldn't get on with your job.'

'That's a relief. The atmosphere is so depressing now. If I can get them outside in the sun, painting again, I'm sure they'll soon forget this nasty business.'

'I shan't,' Reid said. 'I'm hunting a murderer.'

'But it's good riddance to bad rubbish,' Parry objected. 'You really should award a medal to whoever did it.'

Reid's smile was bleak. 'The police aren't allowed to take that attitude, officially. When did you last see George Bullard alive?'

'Ooh!' Parry's hands fluttered again. 'It must have been, let me see ... after dinner I gave a demo. He was there

— somewhat subdued, I thought, if that means anything. Afterwards, he stopped me as I came out of the studio. I was going upstairs to my room — it's private, you understand, otherwise I'd get no rest at all. Someone is always wanting something . . . '

He drew a deep breath. 'Yes, that's when it was. Bullard stopped me in the passage to ask for a private talk.'

Reid leaned forward. 'Did he say what was on his mind?'

'There was no need. Students always want to talk about their work.'

'He said that? Or you assumed it?'

'I see what you mean.' Parry paused, thinking. 'You're right, Inspector, I assumed it. But what else could it have been?'

'If we knew that, it might give us a lead.'

'Well, he didn't turn up, and I didn't worry. He was such a bighead, so full of himself, I was surprised he asked me at all. It's part of my job, of course. But I wonder . . . students do change their minds and panic when it comes down to the nitty-gritty of a personal crit.'

'I wonder too,' Reid said dryly. 'Mrs. Courtney said you'd asked her to do something about Bullard. Mr. Courtney apparently keeps a low profile. Any comments?'

Parry's blue eyes opened wide.

'You suspect me, Inspector. Yes, you do, it's no good denying it! That's wonderful. I can see all that lovely publicity . . . accused has West End show . . . it'll double the price of my pictures!'

'All right, that'll do. I may want to talk to you later, Mr. Parry. I'll see the girl, Snow, next — ask her to come in, will you?'

As the door closed after Keith Parry, Reid looked at Trewin. The constable probably had never had to deal with that sort before.

'Queer, would you say?'

Trewin shrugged. 'Not necessarily. The artistic type.'

'If he is queer, and Bullard needled him . . . well, they blow up, don't they?'

'It's a possibility.'

Reid nodded. 'A distinct possibility. Later on, take a stroll down to the village. See what the locals have to say.'

* ★ *

Miss Eaton moved a chair into the hall and sat opposite the door of the interview room. Sherry jumped onto her lap and settled down, purring happily as Miss Eaton stroked her silky coat.

Together, they watched the faces of the suspects as they were called. Their expressions changed between going in and coming out.

On the way in they were mostly apprehensive. Probably none of them had been interviewed before by the police on a serious matter.

Hilda Keller came out smiling and there was almost a spring in her step.

Sammy Jacobi went directly to the pay-phone and made a call. Long distance, Miss Eaton judged, as he waited to get through. He seemed nervous. Worried? She wondered if he were calling his solicitor.

Fletcher, the Australian, looked thoughtful as if he were meditating on the fact that it was his killing stick that had been used.

Val's face was pale and strained and she came straight to Miss Eaton and said, 'I'm sure the Inspector believes that I murdered Bullard. He was asking why I invited you here. What should I do, Belle?'

'Relax,' Miss Eaton advised. 'I'm not worried, and I'm just as sure you didn't murder anyone.'

Reggie looked gloomier than before as he joined Val and they went off together.

Keith Parry wore an expression of triumph, as if he'd done battle and come out the victor.

Then Linda went in.

7

Which One?

Detective Constable Frank Trewin watched
Reid from the corner of his eye. The big
man in the shiny blue suit had already
sabotaged his image of a Scotland Yard
man. And being called 'constable' all the
time irritated him.

Of course, the London man was
showing the local boy how to run a
murder enquiry . . . well, he wouldn't be
in charge for ever. Reid was close to
retirement age.

When Linda Snow made her entrance,
Trewin took his gaze away from the
Inspector.

The blonde girl paused in the doorway
of the interview room, looking from one
man to the other. She made a tentative
smile. She stood in profile, wearing a thin
tee-shirt, and took a deep breath.

Trewin enjoyed the view. She was about

twenty, he guessed, and knew what she was doing. She was trying it on.

'Please sit down, Miss Snow,' Reid said in a hearty manner.

She closed the door, sauntered into the room and sat opposite the Inspector. She darted a sideways glance at Trewin.

'I don't suppose you liked Bullard any more than the others,' Reid said.

Linda's eyes flashed,

'He was a dirty old man!' Her tone registered indignation. 'Asking me to pose in the nude, at his age. Of course I wouldn't. I'm really shy.'

'I'm sure,' Reid said dryly. 'Last night. Did you see him at any time?'

'Last night I was out with Duke, my boyfriend. We went to a roadhouse — I don't know the name — it's on the way to Penzance.'

'And after that?'

'After that?' Linda looked down demurely. 'I was with Duke.'

'So Bullard didn't worry you much?'

'What d'you think? I've been asked to take my clothes off before.'

'Quite likely. Your boyfriend now, is he

the jealous type?' Reid's voice was deceptively casual.

Linda smiled with satisfaction. 'I can make Duke jealous any time I want . . . he hit George.'

'We'll see what he has to say about that himself. All right, Miss Snow, you can go.'

Trewin watched her leave the room, and eased his collar. 'A sexy piece,' he commented.

'Yes, and she likes to make her boyfriend jealous. Suppose she encouraged Bullard to go too far, and Duke blew up?'

'It's possible, I suppose,' Trewin admitted grudgingly. 'The boyfriend next?'

'I'll save him up. Mr. Keller interests me.'

Wilfred Keller walked briskly into the room and sat down. He was neatly dressed in quality clothes and looked a bit of a dandy.

'D'you mind if I smoke, Inspector?' he asked.

'I don't mind,' Reid said, and waited while he opened a packet of ten cigarettes and lit up from a box of matches.

Trewin wondered about that; a case and lighter in solid gold with a monogram would have seemed more in character.

Reid allowed the silence to linger after he had noted down the Kellers' London address.

'Well now, it appears that your good wife found Bullard's corpse. She claims she was looking for you at the time, which was early this morning. So where were you?'

Keller stared at the glowing end of his cigarette.

'I don't doubt it's true, Inspector. She makes a habit of keeping an eye on me.' He smiled vaguely. 'As it happens, I woke early. I do sometimes in a strange bed. Hilda was still snoring and it seemed a chance to get some sketching done on my own — without an overseer, so to speak.'

He paused to blow a careful smoke-ring.

'I like joining these holiday groups. One gets different tutors, each with his or her own ideas, and sees different kinds of work — most of it not very good, I'm afraid, but still interesting. And, of course a particular view can look different in another light. An early morning light, you know.'

'I don't know,' Reid said mildly. 'So where was this particular view? Up here, at the studio?'

'No!' Keller blurted out the single word. The cigarette trembled in his hand. 'Along the shore.'

'Did you see anyone?'

'I didn't notice.'

'You'd notice young Linda though.'

'Linda?' Keller seemed astonished by the idea.

Reid tried another line of questioning. 'Mr. Parry said you've met before.'

'Yes. On a course in — Warwickshire, I think it was. We — my wife and I — attend so many courses through the summer.'

'That'll do for this time,' Reid said. 'But I may want to see you again.'

Wilfred Keller carefully stubbed out his half-smoked cigarette before he left the room.

Reid said, 'Something there. He's covering up.'

Trewin completed his short-hand notes and suggested, 'Another woman? I mean, his wife has money, but . . . '

'But nothing,' Reid grunted. 'Find out. I'll see — what's her name? Nicholas.'

I'll do all the routine chores, Trewin thought, and he'll grab the credit.

Margo Nicholas swept into the room on a wave of perfume, a one-woman tornado in gypsy finery.

'You'll get nothing out of me, Inspector! Whoever killed George Bullard has my full support and approval. He was a nasty man, a trouble-maker of the worst kind. I'm not surprised that someone killed him — only that it didn't happen long ago.'

'Please sit down,' Reid said, and waited.

'You're entitled to your opinion but, so far as the police are concerned this is an official murder enquiry, and I am duty bound to ask you certain questions.'

'Hardly murder, Inspector. Manslaughter, possibly. Obviously someone lost his temper and hit out. You could call it an accident — even suicide. He certainly asked for it.'

Margo drew a long breath.

'Even if I knew anything, which I don't, I wouldn't tell you. And I hope and believe, neither will anyone else. We're all glad he's dead, so there!'

'The weapon was locked in Mr. Fletcher's car,' Reid said. 'So it can hardly have been someone losing his temper and hitting out, as you suggest. His murder was premeditated.'

His voice hardened. 'And I believe you're a practising psychic. Perhaps you'll go into a trance and ask the spirits to name the murderer for me?'

'Never!'

'I remember your name. There was an enquiry into a death, wasn't there?'

Margo came out of the chair, spitting. She didn't bother to reply, but swept majestically out of the room.

Trewin whistled. 'Bit of a spitfire, that one. An act, do you think, sir? And what was that about a death?'

'We'll dig till we find out,' Reid promised. 'She gave a bad reading and her client committed suicide. We'll give her some rope — and then put the pressure on. Let's have Dickson in.'

Trewin watched 'Duke' Dickson come through the doorway: the effect was halfway between a swagger and a slouch. He wore a leather jacket and oil-stained jeans, his mop of dark hair uncombed.

A tearaway, the constable thought, a yob — and wondered what Linda saw in him.

'Sit down, Dickson,' Reid snapped. 'I've been told that Bullard annoyed your girlfriend and you hit him. Have I got the facts right? Is there anything you want to add?'

'Yeah, he invaded our bedroom too. So I hit him — I don't let anybody mess around with Linda.'

'So perhaps you had another go and hit him too hard?'

'There's no way you're going to pin a murder rap on me. I was never with the boomerang crowd. I like a lay-in when I'm on holiday — so I didn't know anything about that killing stick.'

'Your girlfriend could have told you.'

'But she didn't.'

'We'll see. I want you to account for

your time last evening and night.'

'I took Linda on my bike to a roadhouse. You can check that.'

'We will,' Reid said flatly. 'What time did you leave there?'

'Just before they closed — a bit after eleven, I suppose.'

'On a bike, twenty minutes. That places you here at eleven-thirty — around the time Bullard was murdered.'

'So what? I was with Linda. We came back together and we stayed together. We spent the night together. Try to break that alibi.'

'I don't believe a jury would go a lot on it. Obviously your girlfriend will give you an alibi — we can discount that. Did anyone see you come in? Did you see Bullard?'

'I didn't see anyone. They'd all gone to bed as far as I know. It was dark, with just a light in the hall.'

'But you're insanely jealous about your girl, right?'

Duke took out a knife and began to clean his fingernails. 'You're wasting your time, pig. I didn't kill him.'

Trewin lowered his notepad and half-rose from his seat. 'You'll address the Inspector politely.'

Reid waved him back. 'This laddie doesn't worry me. I've met his type before. Did you hear anything, Dickson?'

'Nothing. This place was as quiet as a morgue.'

Reid studied him in silence. 'All right, you can go — for now.'

'Snotty kid,' Trewin said. 'He needs teaching a lesson.'

'A waste of time, constable. There are too many like that in London, these days — you get used to them. Now suppose Duke and the girl were in it together — '

'I don't fancy Linda as a killer, sir.'

'I don't suppose you do. But don't let a pretty face turn your head.' Reid mused for a while. 'This Bullard seems to have been an obnoxious person altogether.'

'A right bastard,' Trewin said.

'Same difference.'

Reid ticked off Dickson on his list.

'Staff next. There's only one who lives in — the cook. A couple of part-timers to help out. I'll see the cook. You can take

91

care of the part-timers. I doubt they'll know much, if anything, but no stone unturned . . . '

Of course, Trewin thought, the man in charge can't waste his highly-paid time on dull routine.

Mrs. Joyce Willis bustled in and poised on the edge of the chair. She was plump with rosy cheeks, and said: 'I hope this won't take long — I've the lunch to see to.'

'No time at all. As you live in, this is just a formality. We have to question everyone on the premises. It's last night we're interested in — say, from eleven o'clock to after midnight. Did you see anything unusual? Or hear anything out of the ordinary?'

The cook regarded him with scorn.

'Of course not. I'm up early to cook breakfast, so I'm in bed by ten and sleep like a log.'

'George Bullard. Did you ever meet him?'

'Oh, aye, I met him.' For a moment, Trewin thought she was going to spit on the floor. 'We're told not to speak ill of the dead, but that one . . . he'd come into my kitchen and complain about my food. He upset Mrs. Val too. A horrible man.'

'Yes, well . . . everybody seems agreed on that. All right, Mrs. Willis, I don't think I need keep you from your kitchen any longer.'

'That's the lot,' Trewin said. 'One of 'em must have done it — but which one?'

Reid shook his head and looked sadly at him. 'There's still one more. I want to see that private detective, so-called.'

'But she wasn't even here.'

'You know that to be a fact, do you, constable? Eaton was called in to get rid of Bullard . . . so perhaps she did!'

★　★　★

Miss Eaton stroked Sherry as she watched the suspects come out of the interview room. Most likely it was one of them, but which one?

The young blonde girl looked pleased with herself as she crossed the hall and went out into the sunshine.

Wilfred Keller looked apprehensive as

he joined his wife. Something to hide? Miss Eaton wondered. From his wife? Or from the police?

Margo Nicholas was the most interesting. She swept out with high colour, as magnificent as any prima donna leaving the stage.

Duke was making an effort to appear calm, but something in his manner suggested unease.

The cook hurried along the passage towards the kitchen, her lips pressed into a thin line.

Then the red-haired detective opened the door and beckoned to her. Miss Eaton placed Sherry carefully on the chair and went into the interview room. She seated herself with quiet confidence, handbag on her lap and smiled at the inspector.

'This is exciting,' she said conversationally. 'I'm not usually called to a murder.'

'Quite,' Reid murmured. 'More likely divorce, I imagine.'

'Oh, no. You're rather out of date, Inspector. Divorce is so easy these days that private detectives are rarely involved.'

'Mrs. Courtney wanted you to get rid of Bullard, so — where were you last night?'

Miss Eaton opened her handbag and offered a receipt. 'The Combe Tor Hotel.'

'We can check that, you know.'

'Of course, Inspector.'

'What did you plan to do when you got here?'

'There are ways of dealing with awkward customers,' Miss Eaton said pleasantly. She tapped her handbag and switched to her Sam Pike accent.

'A rod can be a great little persuader. Or a beating-up — I'm great at unarmed combat. Some people can be bought off. Or threaten to dig up their past — it's sure amazing how people always have something to hide. I guess it all depends how I sum up a person after meeting them. I like to keep my options open till then. There are ways — even threatening to bring in the law can work sometimes.'

'I wonder why Mrs. Courtney didn't do that?'

'In business, Inspector, people don't like the cops around. It upsets the clients.'

'Too late to mind now,' Reid said. 'You can go — and keep out of my way.'

Miss Eaton rose smoothly and went out of the room, closing the door after her.

Trewin whistled. ' 'I'm great at unarmed combat' . . . I'd like to see her in action . . . and that accent! I'd better check up on her, I suppose.'

'Check on everybody,' Reid said, filling his pipe with a contented air. 'And take an extra long look at the person who found the body. That may not seem fair to you, constable, but it pays, it pays.'

He lit his pipe and drew on it.

'We'll let them relax for a bit, then — '

He made a chopping motion with his hand.

8

Local Newshound

Miss Eaton sat with Val upstairs in the Courtney's private sitting room. It was a large room, furnished with quality antiques; the table was highly polished with a bowl of roses as the centrepiece. Two pictures of the Cornish coast hung on the walls and a hi-fi played softly in the background.

Miss Eaton relaxed with a glass of sherry. The room smelt of roses and polish and had a homely, lived-in feel to it. The Blue Persian lapped contentedly from a saucer. Val was on her second glass.

Val Courtney looked harassed.

'Please don't even think of returning to London tomorrow,' she said. 'When I hired you to take Bullard off my hands, I never dreamed anything like this would happen. It's a nightmare. Business will fall away and we'll be ruined.'

'I doubt it very much,' Miss Eaton said briskly. 'You really must get a grip on yourself, Val. It seems to me much more likely you'll get even more bookings — people do so like to visit the scene of a murder.'

Val shuddered. 'But I don't want ghouls of that sort here! And I'm not happy about the Inspector questioning everyone. It's obvious he doesn't have a clue who did it. It could be anyone — it doesn't have to be someone staying here.'

'No, but it most likely is. And police enquiries have to be thorough — that takes time.'

'But just suppose they never find out, Belle? It'll drag on and on, and we'll always be under suspicion. I couldn't stand that. This business must be settled, one way or the other.'

Val poured herself another sherry.

'Do you remember that awful Tate girl? The Case of the Missing Money, we called it afterwards ... someone was helping herself to our pocket money, and you set a trap and caught her. After we'd dealt with her, she never stole anything again. You were quite the heroine — nobody laughed at your awful American magazines afterwards, I want you to stay and find out who killed Bullard. Will you? Oh, say you will . . . '

Sherry jumped onto Miss Eaton's lap and began to knead. Absently, she stroked the silky fur.

'The Inspector won't like it . . . but then, it would be rather a feather in my cap if I beat him to the murderer, wouldn't it?'

'You'll stay here free of charge of course,' Val said quickly. 'I don't know what your rates are, but we'll meet them somehow — we've got a bit of money put aside for emergencies.'

'All right,' Miss Eaton said. 'I'll do it — for St. Agatha's!'

They both laughed, and the tension eased.

Val said, 'Those were the days. Remember the head girl? What a freak . . . and the rag? Not even you discovered who piled up all the chamber pots outside the games mistress's door. I know you were always keen to be a detective, but how did you get into the business?'

'I pestered all the local enquiry agencies when I left college until I got a start — just handling office routine, of course. Then I switched to another agency, after misrepresenting the work I'd been doing, and got the chance to serve process papers and attend court. After that, I was partnered by an ex-copper to learn the enquiry business and get to know police procedure. In time I worked on my own cases. Then I got lucky and had a big win on the pools — enough to set up on my own — which is what I always wanted, of course.'

Miss Eaton smiled ruefully.

'The first year was a disaster, but I learnt to stand on my own feet and handle my own cases in my own way. A private investigator is all I ever wanted to be. Eventually business picked up and now I'm established and accepted by other agencies in the profession.'

'But why do it at all?' Val asked. 'I mean, it seems so odd.'

'I suppose I'm just curious about

people — and their secrets. They behave so strangely, and everyone has something to hide.'

Miss Eaton put Sherry on the floor and stood up.

'It would be best if I have a room with the students — that'll give me a chance to mix and observe them.'

'Of course. There's no problem — we have a spare room because the Kellers are staying in the village. I'll show you.'

Downstairs, Val led her through the common room — now empty of any police presence — to a passage. One door had been sealed; George Bullard's room.

Miss Eaton asked, 'Who's in which room? I'd better know.'

'First on the left, Sammy Jacobi. Then — ' Val made a grimace — 'the next room was Bullard's. Fletcher, the man with the boomerangs — I can't blame him for what happened, I suppose, but I wish he hadn't come. Bath and loo. The far door leads into the grounds.'

'That's not locked?'

'No. It serves as a fire exit.

'On the right, Duke and Linda. The

second room is yours, the next Margo.'

Val opened the door and Miss Eaton looked into an airy room with two single beds, washbasin and wardrobe, two chairs and a dressing table.

'You're lucky, Belle. You get a double to yourself — now I'll leave you to freshen up for dinner.'

Alone, Miss Eaton walked to the door at the end of the passage and looked out at browning grass and apple trees. There was a path leading around the side of the house. Anyone could come and go, she noted — and if the rooms were empty or people sleeping, without being seen.

She bathed and changed, opened the window wide and joined the painters in the dining room. The small table reserved for staff was empty and the cook was serving.

The atmosphere, which had seemed strained before, was almost cheerful considering that one of their number had been recently murdered.

Miss Eaton suspected the truth hadn't sunk in yet . . . that they were all regarded as suspects by the police . . . except possibly for one person seated around the long table.

As she slid quietly into her seat, Jim Fletcher was retailing a ditty in his flat Australian accent:

'So down in Jones's alley
All the members of the putsch
Laid a dark and dirty ambush
For the bastard from the bush!'

He got a cheer. The jew sitting next to the gypsy-looking woman nudged her in the ribs and laughed.

'That's great, Jim!'

Miss Eaton thought there might be a holiday romance budding there and regarded them kindly.

Linda, the very pretty blonde, was laughing loudly. Her boyfriend, Duke — he hardly seemed the right companion for her — looked surly. Girls today don't seem to know how to choose, Miss Eaton thought; if they ever did, which she doubted.

Margo said, 'Whoever killed George did us all a favour. This is the only cheerful meal we've had since we arrived.'

Joyce smiled as she handed round the

vegetables. 'Yes, we can do without that trouble-maker.'

'Yeah,' Duke added, nodding. 'It saves me the trouble of smashing his face in.'

Linda looked warningly at him. 'You ought to be more careful what you say, Duke. The police might be listening.'

'But it's true,' Margo insisted. 'The atmosphere is different. When the psychic aura is calm, I know I can relax.'

She turned to Miss Eaton. 'You wouldn't believe what we've had to put up with. The air was thick enough to cut with a knife.'

'So I believe,' Miss Eaton said politely, and turned to ask Joyce: 'Don't the Courtneys or Mr. Parry eat with us?'

'Indeed they do, miss, usually — but the Inspector's having a go at them upstairs.'

Fletcher asked, 'I suppose you're another painter come to join our little group?'

'Nope,' Miss Eaton said in her toughest American accent. 'I'm a private eye, and Mrs. Courtney has hired me to find out who killed George Bullard.'

★　★　★

Reid looked casually around the upstairs sitting room. Nicely furnished, and no cheap stuff.

'Drink, Inspector?'

Reid smiled easily. 'I shouldn't, but I will. A small whisky, if you please. All that questioning has given me a thirst. Thanks.'

He sipped slowly, relaxing, enjoying himself. A malt whisky. There must be money in running a studio.

'Are you getting anywhere, Inspector?' Val asked anxiously.

'It's early days yet, Mrs. Courtney. But we're making progress. Information is coming in all the time. We're in touch with the Birmingham police, to see what they can find out about Bullard's background.'

'Then it could be someone who followed him here?'

Reid sipped his whisky, enjoying the warm glow it gave him. He looked from Val Courtney, to her husband, to the tutor.

'I suspect everyone connected with George Bullard until we arrest his murderer. As we shall eventually.'

'I suppose that's good news.'

'What I'm enquiring into at the moment is the financial position of this studio. I get the impression that you don't actually do a lot of business — and money's tight.'

'Someone's been talking,' Reggie said suddenly. 'Who? That's our private business.'

Reid shook his head sadly. 'Wrong, Mr. Courtney. Nothing's private in a murder enquiry. That doesn't mean we go around talking about people's private affairs — but we have to know everything. You appear to have had a substantial sum paid in last winter — '

Parry interrupted. 'That was me, Inspector. I'm not just a paid tutor, but an old friend. I often stay here during the winter months. It's convenient for painting — and gets me away from the commercial grind in London. I knew Reggie and Val were struggling, and put in some money to help out.'

Reid drained his glass. 'Nice of you, Mr. Parry.'

'Why shouldn't I help my friends? I'm quite successful in the commercial art field, and this is a good place to work.'

'No reason why not,' Reid agreed. 'We just like to know these things.'

Reggie Courtney said: 'You think we did it because Bullard might have ruined us, don't you?'

Reid set down his empty glass and stood up to leave. 'The possibility did cross my mind — yes.'

★　★　★

Miss Eaton was up early in the morning and, wearing a track-suit and running shoes, jogged along the cliff path. Below, blue-green sea foamed about jagged peaks of rock. Miss Eaton never dieted; keeping fit was a matter of eating less and taking regular exercise.

She wondered why Bullard's corpse had been left on the lawn when it could so easily have been dropped into the sea, to wash up miles away at a later date. Had the killer been interrupted?

The path wound up and down between bracken and she saw no one. Gulls screeched above a wild and desolate coastline.

When she returned to the studio, she found Jim Fletcher with Linda and Sammy on the lawn, throwing a boomerang.

'Oh, good,' she said, 'Can I have a go?'

'Why not?'

Fletcher demonstrated, then positioned her, and Miss Eaton threw her first boomerang — straight into the ground.

'It's a knack,' he said. 'Keep trying — you'll get it in time.'

Miss Eaton took four throws before she got the curved wood airborne — and observed that Linda had no trouble. When the blonde threw, the boomerang sailed across the sky and returned to her every time.

Sammy was almost as bad as Miss Eaton.

Keith Parry and Margo joined them and the tutor said, 'We can go out painting this morning. The Inspector's given his permission to leave the grounds — but no one's to leave Porthcove, of course.'

'After breakfast,' Margo said. 'Is that the gong? I could eat a horse — this air gives me an appetite.'

Miss Eaton accompanied Jim Fletcher as he put his boomerangs back in his Datsun. It was not a new car and she knew she'd have no difficulty with the lock.

'Is that a killing stick?' she asked, pointing inside. 'May I handle it?'

Fletcher looked gloomy as he reached in and handed her the weapon.

The stick was solid and heavy, slightly crooked. She swung it thoughtfully.

'No need to throw that,' she remarked. 'I told the Inspector so.'

'Did you ought to leave it in your car?'

'Too late to worry. Reckon nobody's going to pinch this one — and there isn't another George Bullard about anyway.'

She saw Parry waiting for them and joined him.

'Keith — I've noticed everyone uses your Christian name — I'd like to join you on your round today. It'll give me the chance to observe each student in turn. I'll just stand in the background while you give your comments.'

'I suppose it'll be all right.' He seemed doubtful.

'Val has asked me to investigate.'

'Oh, I didn't mean that. I meant that some students might be embarrassed having you around while I criticize their work.'

'I'll stay well back,' Miss Eaton promised.

As they went in to breakfast, Parry asked, 'Do you really believe you can find the killer before the police?'

'I doubt it. The police have the organization, but Val wants me to stay, so I shall. I can't just walk out on her when she's in trouble.'

'No, I suppose not.'

Over scrambled eggs, Sammy said, 'The police have searched and sealed George's room. Now they're searching the rest of the house.'

'Whatever for?'

'Who knows? Let's ask our very own

private eye — what do you think, Miss Eaton?'

'I imagine they'll be looking for some link between any one of you and George Bullard.'

'Some hope,' Duke muttered. 'Nobody knew him before he turned up here.'

'That has yet to be proved,' Miss Eaton said mildly. 'It's possible that his killer knew him from somewhere else.'

After breakfast, the students set off with their painting gear and Miss Eaton lingered with Val and Parry over another coffee.

'I give them time to get started on something,' the tutor explained.

'Can you always find them?'

He shrugged. 'Oh, they don't stray far. The usual places — the harbour and cottages, the rocks below the cliffs. They tend to pick the same subjects each time.'

Miss Eaton set off with Parry, sketch-block under his arm and a pocketful of coloured pencils. Just beyond the gate, a battered Ford was parked. One man sat inside, balding, and wearing an old sports jacket with leather patches. He was smoking a cheroot.

When he saw them, he jumped out of the car and tossed his cheroot away.

'I'm Gray,' he said affably. 'Penzance Herald — hope you can spare a few minutes of your time. I'll get your picture in the paper.'

'Certainly not,' Parry said. 'Go away!'

Miss Eaton touched his arm lightly, and murmured, 'Hold on just a moment.' She beamed at the reporter. 'Of course I'll be delighted to talk to you.' She stuck a cigarette in the corner of her mouth and talked around it in her American voice.

'I've been hired to investigate this murder, buddy.'

Gray produced a pencil and notepad. 'Keep talking. Give me some quotes, please — the police won't give me anything.'

'Because they don't know anything.'

'But you do?'

Miss Eaton didn't like it when Gray moved closer; his breath smelled strongly of beer.

'I will,' she corrected. 'I'll nail the killer, you can bet on that. It won't be the first time I've beaten the cops to the draw — stick around, baby, and I'll give you the scoop of a lifetime.'

She blew smoke into Gray's face, forcing him to move back a pace, and quoted her favourite Sam Pike line: 'Crime doesn't pay — not while I'm around.'

'Fascinating.'

'You can inform your readers that Eaton Investigations is on the job — and we never fail!' She pressed a photograph from her handbag into Gray's hand.

As the reporter drove away in a hurry and they continued down the hill, past the tearooms, Parry said in an amused voice, 'I'm amazed. Really I am — you should have been an actress.'

Miss Eaton said briskly, 'It served to draw the newspapers away from Val. And I'm not averse to a little publicity. After all, I'm going to need clients when I return to the office.'

9

With the Painters

Walking down the steep hill, Miss Eaton had a view of the village of Porthcove nestling in the bay. The grey stone walls of the harbour sheltered fishing boats. The sea sparkled in sunlight.

As they reached the bottom of the hill, with the Harbour Inn on one corner and a church on the other, Keith Parry said, 'There's Jim. I'll have a word with him first.'

The sea front was covered with cobblestones worn smooth by time. Fletcher had set up his easel to face a group of fishermen's cottages and his quick sketch looked good to Miss Eaton.

Boldly drawn, with strong contrasts of light and shadow, the pink-washed walls and royal blue window frames were as pleasing to the eye as the actual cottages.

She stood to one side, silent, watching

the Australian's sun-browned face as he stopped work to listen to his tutor's comments.

'You know, Jim, you're almost too good. It's slick. This kind of treatment comes too easily to you.'

Fletcher laughed. 'Guess I've got a commercial outlook. I like to sell my stuff — have to pay my way while I'm travelling.'

'But you've got talent — the possibility of making really good paintings in later years. This way, hacking out routine saleable work, you risk spoiling your chances. Get yourself a technical problem to solve, something you haven't tried before, something that extends you. As I said earlier, try a different medium. Experiment . . . '

'Yeah, why not? You know best, Keith.'

They left Fletcher whistling cheerfully, and moved on. Miss Eaton thought: a confident man. Over-confident, if anything

Parry waved a hand towards the Harbour Inn. 'That's where the Kellers are staying. Do you want a word with Hilda?'

'I'll see her later. It's too nice a day to

spend inside. I think I'm going to enjoy this visit — I've not had much to do with artists before.'

Parry made a face. 'Artists. They aren't so different.'

'I believe you knew the Kellers before they came here.'

'Oh yes, they move around from course to course, a week here, two weeks there. She's got money and believes Wilfred is a genius. She'd do anything to protect him.'

'Even murder?'

Parry didn't reply immediately. After a pause, he said, 'I didn't ought to answer that, did I?'

'But you will. Remember, the police suspect everyone until they make an arrest. That includes you, and Val and her husband. And me.'

'You?' Parry seemed amazed. 'But you weren't here.'

'Val asked me to get rid of Bullard for her. You can bet Reid is checking me just as thoroughly as anyone else.'

'I suppose so, if you put it like that. Well, yes, if Wilfred was threatened, I think Hilda would kill to protect him.

Isn't that what wild animals do? Mother bear with her cub?'

'An interesting comment,' Miss Eaton said as they walked around the harbour.

'There's Wilfred — '

Keller was further along the quay, standing at an easel and laying in a pastel painting on toned paper. He appeared completely absorbed in what he was doing and his sketch of the customs house looked accurate to Miss Eaton.

He heard them moving over the cobblestones and paused to light a cigarette.

'Keith, I wondered when you'd be around. I think I've got something this morning I can work up later.'

Parry compared the sketch with the view.

'Well drawn, as usual. But I think you could emphasize the lights and darks a bit more — the tone values are rather close. It's flat at the moment. Greater contrast would help to get more life into it.'

'I don't want it to look melodramatic,' Keller protested.

'There's no reason it should providing

you don't overdo it. A bit more contrast between the shadows on the building and sunlight on the cliffs behind. You're trying to be too subtle — try cutting out some of the middle greys. I suggest working with a more restricted range of pastels.'

'Well, perhaps. I'll think about it.'

As they walked through the afternoon heat, Miss Eaton wondered why Wilfred Keller bothered to join a painting course if he was reluctant to accept help. She tried to picture him as a cub of Mother bear . . . and wondered if, on some other course, he had met George Bullard.

Parry was smiling. 'Wilfred believes he's better than he really is — and his wife encourages him. He's competent, no more. And I doubt if he ever will be.'

Sammy Jacobi sat on the harbour wall, a box of oil paints in his lap and a small canvas fitted into the lid of the box. He looked down into the harbour at a fishing boat with the name *Jean Michel* on her hull. A man in a blue jersey watched him, spat, and swore in French. His boat looked rather amateurish to Miss Eaton.

'Still struggling with your boats, Sammy?

Why don't you try another subject?'

Jacobi grinned. 'I've got a thing about boats. I just hope I'll improve with practice.'

'Yes, well, boats aren't the easiest things to draw — especially to get them to look as if they're floating in water. Later on, try one that's beached.'

Parry inspected the box of oil paints.

'You've got plenty of paint there, so don't be afraid to use it. At the moment, you're using too much thinner. It isn't water-colour, so lay it on thick and juicy. Try using a palette knife to lay your paint straight from the tube. I want to see some pure colour when I come round next.'

'All right, Keith, I'll have a go. Nice and thick, just as you say.'

Jacobi's paint-box was brand new, Miss Eaton noted, and wondered if he'd ever painted before.

As they left the harbour, Parry remarked, 'Some people will never be much good, but that's not important. If they enjoy painting, they deserve to be encouraged.'

They walked along the shore to where

Linda and Margo were working close together. The sea broke in a froth of foam over blue-veined rocks. Both painters seemed glad to take a rest when their tutor arrived.

He looked at Margo's picture first. To Miss Eaton, it appeared to be a swirl of criss-crossing lines drawn with coloured crayons and blue ink.

Parry said, approvingly, 'Nice one, Margo. I'm pleased to see someone trying something different. Yes, I like it — just carry on the way you're going.'

Miss Eaton looked at the wild eddy of lines intended to represent waves breaking over rocks and thought: she could be a wild card, free with her love — and hate.

Parry turned to the blonde girl.

'Now, Linda, first of all you're attempting something a bit beyond you for the moment. Water-colour is a difficult medium to start with — and the movement of water is not an easy subject for a beginner.'

He clipped his pad to her drawing board. 'Let me show you how to set about it.'

Linda rose from her three-legged stool

and Parry sat down.

Miss Eaton watched, fascinated.

With a few strokes of a soft pencil, he indicated the position of the rocks. He loaded a sable brush with cobalt blue and swept in the sky with a horizontal wash. Quickly mixing ultra marine with some green he covered the sea area. Wiping his brush on a rag, he used the dry brush to wipe out the sea where it foamed over the rocks. The gleaming white of the paper suddenly became spray.

'Like that,' he said, rising. 'Work quickly. Go for the broad masses. Use a large brush, and try one quick sketch after another.'

'That's great,' Linda enthused. 'D'you think I'll ever be able to do anything as good as that?'

'Perhaps in time. It takes a lot of practice — so just keep at it.'

'I will,' Linda said fervently.

And she might be a girl who'd do that, Miss Eaton thought. A girl who'd stay with something — or someone. Like Duke, if she set her mind to save him.

Linda turned to Miss Eaton and asked,

'Are you really a private detective?'

'Sure am.'

Linda sighed. 'It must be an exciting life. I get bored working in an office, just filing and typing.'

'This is the first time I've come up against murder. Usually it's something much more mundane. I think you'd find the waiting and watching just as boring.'

Margo snorted. 'Well, you'll get no help from me. Bullard got what he asked for — and I told the Inspector so.'

'Perhaps that was a bit tactless,' Miss Eaton suggested. 'You're a suspect, like the rest of us.'

'He won't try to pin it on Duke, will he?' Linda asked anxiously.

'Why should he?'

The young girl hesitated, then lowered her voice. 'You see, Duke's been in trouble with the law before. Nothing serious, but — '

Miss Eaton said briskly, 'I don't believe you need worry. Our police don't make a habit of framing the innocent.'

Parry looked at his watch. 'Time for lunch, I think.'

As they left the painters, he added, 'Most students are content with sandwiches at midday. They're keen you know, and want to work straight through. I like to sit at a table and be waited on — it's salad today.'

They came to the road leading up the hill and Miss Eaton said, 'I noticed some steps in the cliff further along.'

'Oh, yes, that's an alternative way up. They come out quite near the studio. but it's a real climb. And if the steps are wet, dangerous. I've been down for an early morning swim in good weather, but I don't advise using them.'

'I'm a good swimmer,' Miss Eaton said.

'If you slip and bang your head on a rock, it won't matter how good a swimmer you are.'

They walked up the hill and, as they reached the tearooms, Parry said, 'There's Hilda — Mrs. Keller.'

Miss Eaton saw Wilfred's wife at a table under a sunshade, looking down at the harbour through a pair of binoculars.

'I'll stop for a word with her, and see you at the house later — '

'Well, don't be late, or you'll upset Joyce. Our cook.'

'Ten minutes at most.'

* * *

Reid drove at a steady speed, the window open and smoking his pipe. His favourite mixture did not give him the usual satisfaction.

The road from Penzance to Porthcove passed through countryside that was a tourist attraction but he saw none of it. He was still waiting for information to come in from a number of different sources, and he had a feeling that this case wasn't going to be an easy one to break.

The feeling annoyed him and, unconsciously, he looked for someone to blame.

Constable Trewin wasn't the ideal man for the job. His lack of experience meant he was probably missing vital leads. On the other hand, he was local and knew the area. Perhaps he'd turned up something by now.

There was that idiot woman, Eaton. A

female private eye with a corny line in Yank dialogue. She didn't help by constantly being underfoot.

Apparently Mrs. Courtney had hired her to find the murderer . . . some hope! Or had she hired her just to get in his way? Reid puffed on his pipe as he considered this idea.

Then there was the reporter, Gray. Reid had nothing against newspapermen when he finalized a case. He enjoyed giving interviews and seeing his name in the paper — at the end of a successful case.

But was this one going to be a success? He had his doubts about that.

With only a few months to go to retirement, he'd bought a house and could look forward to a decent pension. All he needed was one successful case so he could retire in a blaze of glory.

He knocked out his pipe as he pulled up outside the Porthcove Studios. This case wasn't going to be the one he wanted. Well, he had a fall-back position. He could ease himself out and leave Trewin to carry the can.

★   ★   ★

As Parry continued up the hill in long-legged strides, Miss Eaton approached Mrs. Keller and took the empty seat beside her.

Wilfred's wife was a large woman running to fat. Her clothes were fashionable and expensive, her perfume discreet. But she was older than her husband and her rather plain face had the hint of a moustache.

'Mrs. Keller. I'm Miss Eaton, a private investigator. Valerie Courtney has retained me to look into the death of George Bullard, and I'm hoping you can help me.'

Mrs. Keller lowered her binoculars, sipped from a cup of tea and daintily nibbled at a fresh cream cake.

'I know nothing whatever about it.'

'You discovered the body.'

'By chance. As I told the Inspector, I was looking for Wilfred.'

'He's a wandering eye, has he?' Miss Eaton managed to get a note of sympathy into her voice.

'I do sometimes wonder. I've never actually caught him with another woman — but he does go missing from time to time. Of course, it may all be perfectly innocent. He is keen on his painting.'

She waved her binoculars.

'These are good for more than watching the feathered variety. From here, I have a good field of observation. I can keep an eye on him — and that blonde girl.'

'Quite,' Miss Eaton said, and decided to bring her own binoculars here. It was an ideal vantage point from which to observe the painters down below.

She turned in her seat and looked up the hill. The roof of the studio and the top row of windows only were visible.

'Oh, yes,' Mrs. Keller said. 'Only the other day I noticed somebody appear at one of the upstairs windows. I couldn't make out who it was.'

Miss Eaton wondered. There weren't many people it could have been. Val or Reggie, Joyce the cook. Presumably Parry would have been out with his students.

'Which day?' she asked. 'At what time of day?'

Mrs. Keller looked astonished. 'That's interesting — it simply hadn't occurred to me before. It was the day before yesterday — and yesterday I found that awful man's body on the lawn. It seems years ago. In the afternoon it was, I remember now.'

I'll check with Val, Miss Eaton thought, and said, 'I don't believe you have to worry about young Linda. She seems completely wrapped up in her boyfriend.'

Mrs. Keller snorted.

'A most unsuitable type for a young lady to associate with. But, to be fair to him, nowhere near as bad as Bullard. I'm glad he's dead. He ran down Wilfred's pictures, you know.'

'He seems to have run down everyone.'

'Wilfred was with me during the evening and night,' Mrs. Keller stated firmly. 'In case you're wondering. It was in the early morning he went out sketching.'

Yes, Miss Eaton decided, Parry was right; she was rather like a mother bear who would kill to protect her cub. And just how early had Wilfred left her bed?

She said, 'I'm off to lunch,' and started

up the hill at a brisk pace.

When she reached the studio, she passed through the common room to reach her own room. She met Detective Constable Trewin in the passage and he looked curiously at her.

'Miss Eaton,' he said, 'I've just searched your room on the Inspector's orders.'

'I don't doubt it. And every other room too, I imagine. At least, that's what I'd do in your shoes.'

He smiled, and she thought he had a pleasant smile under his mop of ginger hair. His face had a freshly scrubbed appearance that made him look very young.

'You're right, of course. Confidentially, your bourbon smells peculiar.'

'I don't like the stuff,' Miss Eaton confessed. 'It's really apple juice — but the bottle is good for my image.'

Trewin grinned.

'You'll notice the hair next to the latch on your suit-case has been disturbed. Did you think I wouldn't notice it?'

'Oh, no.' Miss Eaton said. 'I'd expect a

professional to notice. But — have you forgotten? — there's a murderer around somewhere. And I doubt if he or she, is a professional.'

For a moment, Constable Trewin looked disconcerted.

10

Private Investigations

Lunch was ham salad with Val, Reggie and Keith Parry, taken at the small table in the dining room.

Miss Eaton said, 'Mrs. Keller told me she saw someone at a front upstairs window of this house the afternoon before Bullard was killed.'

'That's odd,' Val said, and frowned. 'I was shopping in Penzance.'

'Not me,' Reggie said, helping himself to another slice of ham. 'I was down at the harbour buying fish for dinner.'

Parry poured water from a jug into a glass. 'That's right — I remember seeing you. I was there too, with the students. How peculiar. Is anything missing?'

Val Courtney and Reggie looked at each other.

'I haven't noticed anything.'

Reggie laughed. 'Of course! She saw

Joyce — there isn't anyone else it could be.'

Miss Eaton questioned the cook when she brought their dessert from the kitchen.

'It wasn't me,' Joyce declared. 'I was resting on my bed, and my room's at the back of the house.'

Parry said, 'So Mrs. Keller must have imagined it.'

'Unless you had an intruder. Would there have been anyone in the grounds?'

'Only Bert, our part-time gardener. But he wouldn't go into the house.'

'I'll ask him,' Miss Eaton said.

After coffee, she fed Sherry and strolled into the grounds behind the studio. Bert had the deliberate movements of a countryman as he weeded between rows of vegetables. A wide-brimmed hat shielded his neck from the sun.

When Miss Eaton posed her question, he took his time answering.

'In the afternoon, Miss? I do remember they was all out. Only me here — and the cook. Nobody else in the house that I know of.'

132

'Was anyone in the grounds?' Miss Eaton asked patiently. 'Did you see anyone at all.'

'Only the gent painting. Didn't see nobody else. Quiet, it was.'

'Do you know which painter it was?'

'No, Miss. I see 'em around, but I don't know any of them by name.'

'Keith will probably know,' Miss Eaton said. 'Thank you.' She went back to the house.

In the hall, Val had opened the art shop to provide the tutor with a new sketch pad. Inspector Reid was speaking to her as Miss Eaton arrived.

'The fact is, Mrs. Courtney, anyone in this house — anyone at all — could have murdered Bullard. Surely that is obvious? Now, if I may have your cooperation — '

'Stop bullying her,' Miss Eaton said crisply. 'Of course Val didn't do it, Inspector — she's an old girl of St. Agatha's!'

Reid looked sour. 'That means nothing to me.'

'Keith,' Miss Eaton said. 'I've just spoken to Bert and he told me that someone was painting in the garden that afternoon. Can you remember who it was?'

'Of course!' Parry struck his forehead with the heel of his palm. 'How did I forget that? It was George — he said he wanted to paint flowers. He was on his own here all afternoon.'

'What's this?' Reid demanded. 'Bullard? Something you forgot to tell me?'

Parry repeated his story for the Inspector, who grunted. 'I don't see how that gets us anywhere.'

'So it could have been Bullard that Mrs. Keller saw at the window?' Miss Eaton said.

'But why should he go upstairs? The upper floor's private — all the students know that.'

'Exactly. If it was Bullard, it gives us another light on his character.'

'But nothing's missing,' Val protested.

'So what was he doing?'

'Snooping?'

Miss Eaton heard Duke's bike and walked outside and around the side of the house to the car park. He was taking off his crash helmet, releasing a mop of unruly black hair as she approached.

'Cops still here?' he asked.

'The murder team's finished and left. Reid and Trewin are still around.'

Duke pulled a face. 'Well, I took a ride to get away from them — I can't stand the pigs poking their noses into my affairs.'

'Linda mentioned that you'd had some trouble with the police before.'

He scowled. 'Linda wants to keep her mouth shut. It was nothing anyway. Just a bit of a dust-up.'

'The police will dig it up, you can be sure,' Miss Eaton warned. 'They'll be looking into the backgrounds of everyone here.'

'And they'll pick on me,' Duke said savagely.

'They treat everyone as a suspect.'

'Yeah? Well, me and Linda alibi each other.'

Miss Eaton ignored this, and said, 'I heard that you hit Bullard.'

'So what? He was annoying Linda.'

And you might easily have hit him

again, Miss Eaton thought — and too hard a second time.

She asked; 'How do you get on with Keith? He spends some time with her.'

'Him? Bit of a pansy, I'd say. But he's strong enough — he pulled me off Bullard with no effort.'

'They often are,' Miss Eaton said absently.

Reggie Courtney caught up with Parry just as he was setting off down the hill to join his students.

'Hi, Keith. Just a minute.'

Parry paused. 'You're looking worried, Reggie. What's up?'

'I am worried. What's going to happen? The police have searched the whole house . . . and Bullard. Do you know anything about him?'

'Not a thing,' Parry said cheerfully. 'Look. Reggie, I must rush now or the paying customers will wonder when they're going to get any help. Just stop worrying. The police will fade away in time and everything will soon be back to normal.'

Courtney said gloomily, 'I doubt if

anything will ever be normal again.'

'See you this evening at dinner.'

With a casual wave, Parry strode off down the hill towards the harbour. He whistled an old Beatles' number.

★ ★ ★

Miss Eaton found Val Courtney working on her accounts in the office.

'Sorry to interrupt, but I want to take a look at everybody's room.'

Val looked harassed. 'Must you? Oh, I suppose so — the police have already been through the house, you know.'

'And obviously not found anything. But I suspect they were looking for a direct link between Bullard and someone he might have known previously. I just want to get a better feel for the people involved — and their room can tell a lot about a person's character.'

'Whatever you say, Belle. I just want this business cleared up so we can get back to the way we were before.'

'It would be best if you come with me.' Val closed her account book and pushed it aside. 'All right then. I don't suppose any of the doors are locked, but I'd better get my keys.'

They went through the common room and Val opened the first door on the left. 'Jacobi,' she said shortly.

Sammy was a messy person at home, Miss Eaton observed. Discarded clothing lay across an unmade bed. There was a smell of oil paint and turpentine; half-used paint tubes littered the dressing table.

Bullard's room came next; still locked and sealed by the police.

'Fletcher,' Val announced.

This was a tidy-room where everything was neatly arranged. Miss Eaton saw a portable typewriter in its case and remembered that the Australian did some writing. An organized man, she thought; ready to take off at a moment's notice.

Margo Nicholas's room was opposite. Here the smell of perfume was strong, and a pack of tarot cards were stacked on the table. All her clothes had been put away and the bed made; the washbasin had been cleaned. There was a lot of cheap jewellery in one of the drawers.

Miss Eaton passed by her own room and looked into that shared by Duke and Linda. There were bike and girlie magazines on one side of the double bed; a handbook on painting on the other. The room smelt of tobacco with the window shut; old cigarette stubs filled the ashtray. Linda carried a lot of make-up and a selection of exotic underwear.

'Do you want to go upstairs?' Val asked.

'Yes please. Just a minute . . . '

Miss Eaton went outside and around the house to look in through the window of George Bullard's room. She saw an oil painting of red roses in a sunlit garden; probably the last thing he painted. She studied it closely but, apart from impressing her as a nice painting of roses, it told her nothing. His clothes and paints had been put out of sight and the bed was made.

She rejoined Val, and they went upstairs.

'This is Keith's room.'

Miss Eaton saw a long room, one end of it stacked with canvases, an easel and a table with paints and brushes. The other end contained a bed and wooden chest and an armchair. Shelves held an impressive number of large art books and there were colour reproductions of famous modern paintings on the walls.

'Quite a library,' Miss Eaton commented.

'Keith gives talks to various groups. He needs a lot of research material handy.'

And he liked bright clothes, Miss Eaton noted. One window looked out on the lawn and goldfish pond.

The cook's room was small and neat, at the back of the house. There were a couple of cigarette ends in an ashtray on the windowsill, half-hidden by a curtain. The wardrobe contained a surprising number of smart dresses.

'Good clothes,' Miss Eaton remarked.

'Oh yes, our Joyce keeps her looks. Must be the Cornish air. When she dresses up on her day off, you wouldn't know her.'

'I've seen your room of course, Val — how long have you been here?'

'It must be . . . getting on for twelve years. I suppose you'll be visiting the Kellers?'

Miss Eaton nodded. 'Yes indeed. I'll just take a walk down there now.'

11

Customs and Excise

Miss Eaton walked slowly down the hill as far as the tearooms. She selected an outside chair beneath a sunshade and ordered a pot of tea.

While she waited, she studied the harbour and seashore through her binoculars. She had a clear view of the boats in the harbour and the fishermen's cottages. She could pick out individual painters and the sweep of the sandy bay and gulls swooping over crags of rock.

After her tea arrived, she turned around to view the studio above her. The upper row of windows showed up plainly. She watched them closely and decided Mrs. Keller was telling the truth when she said she hadn't been able to recognize the person she had seen. She reminded herself it was still only an assumption that this person had been George Bullard.

As she drank her tea, she considered her suspects — and had to admit they were all equally suspect. Even the staff could not be eliminated. Reggie was obviously worried. Parry? Bullard would most likely have spent more time needling the tutor than anybody else. But surely an experienced tutor — and he was that; she'd observed for herself that he was good at his job — could handle one awkward student without losing his temper?

It was impossible to see Joyce in the role of murderer. Val? Ridiculous . . . Miss Eaton smiled as she recalled the number of times Sam Pike had found himself at the wrong end of a gun held by the woman who had hired him. The situation had become a cliché in American pulp detective stories.

She could recall one passage from *Bootleg Blonde*:

I turned, and my raven-haired client held a gun in her hand. It was pointed at me, and her face had grown hard and cruel, like a death mask with frostbite.

'This is the pay-off, shamus,' she sneered.

I grabbed for my own rod as she squeezed the trigger. I heard the click of the hammer coming down on an empty chamber — natch, I'd emptied it when she went to the powder room — and then I was pumping lead into that gorgeous body . . .

Loyally, Miss Eaton put the idea from her. An old girl of St. Agatha's? Never!

She drained her second cup of tea and continued down to the Harbour Inn. It was after closing time and customers were coming out. She walked into a cosy bar festooned with nets and illuminated in red and green from ships' lanterns.

One of the last to leave the bar, she noted, was vaguely familiar — a man in a blue jersey. Then she remembered he had been aboard the French fishing boat.

The landlord called, 'Sorry, miss, but we're closed.'

Miss Eaton smiled. 'I'm calling on Mrs. Keller. Is she in her room?'

He nodded. 'First door on the left at the top of the stairs.'

She went up quickly and tapped on the door. Hilda Keller opened it.

'It's me again. We met at the tearooms before lunch — could I come in and speak with you for a moment?'

'I suppose so — providing you don't smoke.' Hilda's tone of voice was grudging. 'I can't stand the smell of cigarette smoke — I've only just cured Wilfred of the habit.'

'I promise I shan't smoke.'

'I've already had the police here searching. It's quite ridiculous. Neither Wilfred nor I had ever set eyes on the man before we came here.'

The room was a double, with a wide bed, large armchairs and an old-fashioned wardrobe; a room for people who could afford to pay extra in the season. Windows overlooked the harbour, framed by lace curtains stiff with starch. They were wide open and a smell of seaweed and the screeching of gulls came in.

Miss Eaton saw a selection of expensive cosmetics on the dressing table, a lacy black nightdress folded neatly on a pillow. One of Wilfred's pastel pictures was propped up on a chair.

She perched on the edge of an

armchair and looked around.

'Yes?' interrogated Mrs. Keller sharply. 'What is it you wanted to see me about?'

'I wondered if you had much to do with the other painters on Wilfred's course.'

'As little as possible. We try to keep to ourselves. Such common types, I always think — except for James. He seems truly to appreciate Wilfred's work. It's even possible he'll be able to arrange a London exhibition. A bit of a rough diamond, I fancy, but a cut above the others.

'The jew is polite but . . . really I mean, one can't possibly allow oneself to be involved with a tradesman. As for that dreadful lout in the leather jacket — so unsuitable for such a pretty girl — his fingernails are black! And that awful woman smothered in cheap scent and artificial jewellery . . . well, really.'

Snob, Miss Eaton thought, and said, 'I do like this painting of your husband's. So nice to be able to recognize the subject — and the boats do look as if they're floating in water.'

'Yes. He's very good and one day the

146

critics will admit it. Real painting, I'm glad to say, is coming back into fashion after all that abstract rubbish.'

Mrs. Keller fingered her moustache and said, abruptly. 'I'm thinking of leaving here. I've told Wilfred — he can't afford to get mixed up with a murder. Bad for his reputation.'

'The police won't allow that I'm afraid,' Miss Eaton said mildly. 'In their view you are both suspects.'

'Suspects!'

'Yes. Can you remember which window it was where you saw the intruder?'

'Window? Window . . . the last one at the end. On the right-hand side of the house.'

'Could you make a guess please? Did the figure look more like a man, or a woman?'

'Does it matter?' Mrs. Keller asked irritably. 'I couldn't tell — it could have been either. Now, if you've finished . . . ?'

'Oh, yes, I've finished,' Miss Eaton said sweetly. 'But the police haven't. I do recommend that you keep yourself available if you wish to avoid trouble.'

She went downstairs and out into the sunshine, thinking: the last window on the right was in Keith Parry's room.

She strolled along the stone quay, looking at the boats. The French fishing boat was still in harbour but she saw no sign of the man in the blue jersey. Sammy, she noted, had moved further along the quayside to try his hand at drawing a boat that had been hauled up out of the water.

As she stood there, enjoying the view, a man in uniform bustled up. His voice had a snap to it and his words poured out in a quick gabble, as if they were all joined together.

'I am an officer of the Customs and Excise and it is my duty to ask if you have taken anything from any boat? Do you object to my searching your handbag?'

Miss Eaton was taken aback. 'Do you have some identification?'

The fussy little man produced an official-looking card in a plastic wallet.

She looked closely at it, and replied, 'No objection.'

She watched his face as he opened her

handbag and found the Smith and Wesson. He looked startled and held it gingerly.

'It's only a replica,' she informed him kindly.

He looked relieved, went through her bag more cautiously and handed it back.

'Where do you come from?'

'London.'

'Are you intending to stay long at Porthcove?'

'A few more days. I'm with Val Courtney, up the hill at the studio.'

'I see. An artist.' He paused. 'But you're not painting . . . '

'I'm not an artist. I'm an old school friend of Mrs. Courtney.' An idea began to form in Miss Eaton's head. She smiled and asked pleasantly, 'Is there much smuggling here?'

'A little, sometimes. But, of course, they don't always sail into harbour. This is a routine check. We keep an eye on foreign boats — and anyone lingering near them.'

'Like me. Well, thanks . . . '

From the harbour, Miss Eaton walked

around the headland and along the shore. She walked quickly, ignoring the heat. She was excited.

Smuggling. Suppose Bullard had been involved? Or had he stumbled on a gang by chance? That would provide a strong motive for murder.

She'd never been happy with the idea that someone was sufficiently upset by Bullard's barbed remarks to actually kill him. Unless, as in Duke's attack, they simply lashed out in anger. But the killing stick had been locked away in Jim's car — and that meant premeditation.

She reached Parry, where he was commenting on Margo's latest effort — a study of the cliff face — and paused to ask:

'Is anything missing from your room, Keith? Anything moved, or out of place?'

He raised an eyebrow. 'Not that I've noticed. I don't keep much of value there anyway — apart from my paintings, that is. Why?'

'Mrs. Keller seems sure it was at your window that she spotted the intruder.'

Parry laughed. 'Always assuming she

didn't imagine it. But I'll take a closer look now that you mention the matter.'

Miss Eaton continued along the sand until she reached the steps cut into the face of the cliff and started up. It was a steep climb and the steps were narrow; obviously they would be dangerous in wet weather. But a quick way up or down for smugglers.

She wondered about Wilfred and Hilda. Staying at the Inn by the harbour made them strong suspects. Suppose Bullard had seen something and tried blackmail? Or he could he have been one of the gang and tried a double-cross? Could there be a second gang involved? A hi-jack?

She reached the top of the steps and the cliff walk, and could see the studio not far away.

What was being smuggled? Marijuana? Something small presumably. Gems?

A memory nagged at the back of her mind, something she had read recently but couldn't recall immediately. She felt annoyed with herself. It was something she would have to check out.

When she arrived at the studio, she used the pay-phone in the hall to call Geary in Birmingham. He was a private investigator she'd used before to save herself a journey to the Midlands.

'Mr. Geary? Miss Eaton. I need some background on George Bullard — '

'Don't tell me you've got yourself mixed up in murder, Isabel?' Geary chuckled.

'I've been retained to investigate.'

The voice on the phone became serious. 'Well, look after yourself. There's a killer loose — and it's a police job anyway. What d'you want to know?'

'Anything you can get me quickly. His job. Was he married? Who benefits? His style of living, just general background stuff.'

She gave the number of Porthcove Studios.

'Try to get back to me tomorrow, will you?'

'I'll try — and you owe me one.'

Miss Eaton got into her Fiat and drove away. She turned onto the main road and put her foot down. In Penzance, she stopped once to ask the way to the Public Library. She found the reading room and began to go through back issues of the *Daily Independent*, searching for that elusive memory.

She turned pages, scanning rapidly, going back day by day until —

GREAT DIAMOND THEFT

'A daring robbery was carried out in Amsterdam yesterday, when diamonds estimated to be worth a quarter of a million pounds were stolen from the House of Hertman.

'A police spokesman said that so far no trace of the thieves or the missing gems had been found, but several lines of enquiry were being pursued.

'It is thought that the diamonds may already have been smuggled out of the country . . . '

Miss Eaton sat back in her chair with a feeling of satisfaction. Diamonds, worth a fortune, smuggled out of Holland — and into Porthcove? It was possible, she decided.

She made brief notes, returned the file of newspapers and went out to her car. As she drove back to the studio, her thoughts revolved around the reward offered for information leading to the recovery of the stolen gems.

She parked the Fiat and hurried around the corner of the house, knowing she was late for dinner. She saw Sherry on the lawn, crouched beside the pond and trying to hook out the fish with her paw.

'Sherry! Stop that!'

The Persian looked around guiltily as Miss Eaton crossed the grass. Goldfish swam peacefully in green water, big fat goldfish . . .

An old Sam Pike novel, *Shroud For A Stripper*, flashed into her mind. Sam was on the trail of a ransom in emeralds and no one seemed to know where they were hidden. He was interviewing one of the suspects . . .

She was stacked like a card-sharp's deck — and kept goldfish?

I reached into the tank and scooped out one of the smaller fish lying on the bottom. The reddish-gold body squirmed in my hand and I felt something hard under the flesh. I took out my knife and slit open the fish — a sparkling green emerald tumbled out.

Mary-Jo came at me like a hopped-up tarantula, and I stuck the knife in her . . .

Miss Eaton knelt on the grass beside the pond and thrust her hand underwater. She caught one of the fish and felt it gently. Soft. She put it back and tried another, and another.

Beside her, Sherry purred in ecstasy. Miss Eaton had probably tried most of the goldfish before she gave up. No diamonds.

Sherry looked at her with a disgusted expression.

Miss Eaton arrived late for dinner, which she had alone.

'Sorry I'm late, Joyce. I had to go into Penzance. Where is everyone?'

'That's all right, Miss. Val and her husband are upstairs. Mister Keith is in the studio, giving one of his demonstrations.'

'That might be interesting,' Miss Eaton said.

After her meal, she took her coffee into

the studio and found an empty stool at the back of the room.

Parry had a medium-sized canvas on an easel and oil paints laid out on a small glass-topped table. On a second easel was a sketch — squared-up — of the cottages by the harbour.

As she settled herself, Parry was saying, 'Obviously I don't have time to carry this through to a finish in one session. What I propose to show you is how to start off building up a studio picture from your holiday sketch. Something you can try at home on winter evenings.

'This is an old canvas I'm using again. I just slapped a coat of primer on and squared-up. It's something you can do to save buying new canvas all the time. So . . . '

With a stick of charcoal, he drew in the main lines of the composition.

'Nothing too elaborate. Just guide lines to place the subject. Now, first of all, I want to get rid of the white — that helps to relate tones. The overall colour of the sky is blue, so I use cobalt with plenty of turps and a large brush.

'Using the same blue but adding a touch of black, and a dash of white I lay in the cliffs. For the cottages I add an ochre.'

Was he looking at her? Miss Eaton wondered. Surely he didn't object to her attending his demonstration? No, hardly; he was smiling as he worked.

'Now we have the canvas covered,' Parry continued, 'and the overall tone makes it easier to work on. I'm using a smaller brush to sketch in the cottages. It's worth taking some time over this, to get your drawing right.'

She studied the faces of his students as he worked. They appeared absorbed in the lesson. No one was worrying about her, or George Bullard, or his killer.

'Next, block in the main masses, light against dark, dark against light. Use the same colours, but thicker now. A hint of pink in the cottage walls. A touch of white to indicate cloud and break up the sky and show an aerial perspective. Some dark in the foreground — this also helps with perspective.'

He paused. 'That's as far as I'll take it this time. Obviously I can continue later and probably will. But it's enough to show you how to set about building up a painting from one of your holiday sketches.'

As he began to clean and wipe his brushes, the class crowded around the canvas to see it close up.

Linda asked about squaring-up.

'I should have explained that, Linda. It makes the drawing easier, if you transfer what is in one square in your sketch, to the corresponding square on canvas.'

Miss Eaton asked casually, 'Did you get the chance to look around your room, Keith?'

'Yes, I did. Nothing's missing, and nothing appears to have been touched.'

* * *

Detective Constable Frank Trewin leaned comfortably against the bar counter of the Harbour Inn. It was after licensing hours and he was alone with the landlord. Reid had gone back to Penzance and left him to deal with the local — and routine — enquiries.

Ah, well, Trewin thought, cuddling a free pint of best bitter, there was something to be said for being left alone to get on with the job in your own way.

Calling to the landlord, he allowed his Cornish burr to show in his speech.

'You know me, Mr. Oakes. I'm a local man. You can say what you like and it'll go no further.'

'Aye, up to a point — but remember this is my livelihood, Frank. I can't afford to scare my customers away.'

'No fear of that. Just a hint is all I want. Tell me something about the Kellers. Who comes to see them? Do they get on together? Anything about them you think I ought to know. Remember, this is a murder job.'

Oakes removed his spectacles and polished them absently. 'Not much to tell — they keep to themselves pretty much. She's got the money and likes her comfort — bit of a snob, I'd say. He's mad about painting, and she encourages him.'

He sipped a small whisky. 'Visitors? Well, that chap I hear got himself killed

159

was in one evening. Downright rude he was. The Kellers went up to their room pretty quick.

'Then there was the Aussie — tell him by his accent — he seemed to get on well enough with them. Took a few drinks, he did, but Aussies are like that — pour it straight down they do — comes of their peculiar licensing hours I suppose. Shocking way to treat good beer.

'And there was that spinster woman staying with Mrs. Courtney. She's no painter — she called for a chat with Mrs. Keller one day.'

'Did she now?' Trewin straightened his lanky body. If a private eye was mixing in police business, she'd have to be warned off. Murder was a serious matter.

'How about the studio people? Mrs. Courtney and her husband? The tutor?'

Oakes finished his whisky, washed the glass and began to dry it.

'Don't see much of the Courtneys during the season, though Reggie looked in a few days back. Keith will stop for a drink sometimes. In winter, it's another matter. Mostly it's Reggie Courtney and

160

that tutor of theirs — reckon they're old friends, those two.'

Trewin's ears pricked up.

'Queer, you mean?'

'Wouldn't surprise me if Keith was. But not Reggie — no, I didn't mean it that way. Just old pals.'

'Interesting,' Trewin said, draining his glass.

12

Unlikely Allies

Margo looked on with some amusement as Jim Fletcher patiently picked up the boomerang that Sammy had failed to get airborne. He handed it to Linda, and said:

'Watch how this sheila does it. Watch her wrist as she throws.'

Linda made her throw and Jim, Sammy and Keith watched. She was wearing tight jeans and a thin tee-shirt and it wasn't her wrist they were watching.

Margo shook her head slightly and brass earrings jangled. They were wasting their time. She recognized Linda's type; a one-boy girl, no matter what. She was disappointed in Sammy.

'What an action!' Fletcher exclaimed. 'Again, Linda.'

But before the blonde could throw again, Duke Dickson came around the corner from the car park, and he was angry.

'Somebody used my bike last night! Come on, own up — who was it? The tank's nearly empty!'

Linda paused, boomerang in hand. 'But you were going to fill it, Duke. Perhaps you forgot.'

'I didn't forget. It cost me a tenner only yesterday.'

Margo's memory stirred. 'I thought I heard a bike when I woke up last night. Early this morning, I should say. I didn't think much of it at the time — I suppose I assumed it was you.'

'It wasn't me. It must have been somebody here — and they should have filled the tank for me.'

Fletcher drawled, 'Maybe there's no all-night garage around here.'

'Why would anyone want to use it in the middle of the night anyway?' Sammy asked.

'Whoever it was, is going to pay for the petrol,' Duke said grimly.

'I suppose it could be some local kids joy-riding,' Parry said. 'Though we've never had that sort of trouble before.'

'If I catch 'em, you won't have it again!'

★   ★   ★

Hilda Keller sat at the dressing table in their bedroom at the Harbour Inn. She massaged a new and expensive face cream into her skin as she watched Wilfred in the mirror. He was getting his sketching gear together.

'Have you started smoking again, Wilfred?'

'No, dear. You'll always smell cigarette smoke in a hotel room.'

Hilda let it pass.

'I think we ought to leave, Wilfred. That woman detective was here yesterday and practically accused us of being suspects — '

'We are, dear.'

Hilda looked at her husband.

'Did you kill that dreadful Bullard person, Wilfred? I'd quite understand — he deserved to die. I must know so that we get our story straight. An alibi? Is that the word? And, of course, I'll stand by you. I'll hire the most expensive lawyer.'

Wilfred looked startled. 'I assure you that I haven't killed anyone.'

'Then we'll leave today.'

'That wouldn't be a good idea. The police wouldn't like it, dear. To them, we should look guilty, d'you see? No, we must stick it out.'

Hilda pressed her lips into a firm line and took a deep breath.

'So you don't want to leave? Is, there another woman?'

Wilfred sighed. 'Of course not, dear. Let's go down to breakfast. You'll feel better after you've eaten.'

★ ★ ★

Miss Eaton arrived at a trot, completing her morning jog along the cliff path. She crossed the lawn to the boomerang throwers.

'What now?' she asked, looking from one to another.

'Another mystery for you,' Linda said, and smiled.

'Someone used my bike last night,'

Duke broke in angrily.

'Where is it?'

Miss Eaton followed Duke around the side of the house to the car park. The Kawasaki was propped up against the wall.

She placed her hand on the engine. 'Cold.'

'The tank's almost empty.'

'You didn't lock it?'

'I didn't think there was any need to here.'

'I wonder who it could have been,' Miss Eaton murmured. 'And why?'

'When I find out, they'll hand over a tenner. And I don't care why they took it.'

They went in to breakfast. No one admitted to borrowing the motorcycle, and Miss Eaton mentioned the matter to Val Courtney.

Val asked Duke, 'Are you going to tell the police?'

'What for? They wouldn't believe me anyway.'

After breakfast, Val opened the shop for anyone needing materials. Sammy was first in line.

'A large tube of white,' he said. 'And ochre, cobalt and ultramarine. I'd better have a green too. It's Keith — he wants me to use a palette knife, so I'm going to need a lot of paint.'

He began to grumble in a good-natured way. 'This painting lark is costing me a bomb!'

Val smiled. 'It's good for business anyway — Keith knows what he's doing.'

Sammy chuckled. 'You can say that again!'

Miss Eaton waited till all the students were served and had gone on their way; then she said, 'I want to talk to Joyce. Do you know if she smokes?'

'She's in the kitchen,' Val said. 'And no — few cooks smoke. It spoils their taste buds.'

Miss Eaton nodded and walked along the passage to the kitchen. Joyce was stacking dirty crockery near the washing machine, ready for the part-time help. Sherry was attacking a bowl of fish as if she were starving.

'Ah, that's where she's got to. I might have known.' Miss Eaton beamed at the cook. 'Sherry's got her head screwed on — she makes friends with the cook wherever we stay.'

'A beautiful cat,' Joyce said.

'Did you see anything of Bullard on his last afternoon? Did he ever try making a pass at you?'

'Bullard?' Joyce appeared astonished. 'Never!' She flourished a carving knife. 'A good thing he didn't, after insulting my cooking. I'd have used this on him!'

Miss Eaton strolled outside as Reid drove up, looking for Trewin. She waited on the lawn, studying the house as an old Ford arrived with a rattle and a bang.

Gray, the local reporter, got out, smoking a cheroot. He seemed in high spirits as he thrust a copy of the *Herald* at her.

'Here, read all about yourself. Any more copy for me? The local coppers aren't giving much away.'

He winked. 'Keep me in touch, won't you? Any tips you provide mean a story for me — and publicity for you.'

'When I get something, you're welcome.'

Miss Eaton took a pace back as he edged closer, breathing out beer fumes.

'I've been doing a spot of digging myself, so maybe I've got a lead for you. That character staying at the Inn — '

'Keller?'

'Yes, him. He's a local man. And he had a girlfriend before she got married to someone else.' Gray grinned slyly. 'You've met her — here. Joyce Willis, your cook. Maybe he came back to see his old flame — what d'you think?'

'So it was Wilfred,' Miss Eaton murmured. 'Thanks for the tip.'

'I can't stop now,' Gray said. 'There's been a burglary at Red Wheal — Jarvis's place. I'm on my way to cover it now. See you around.'

The reporter hopped back into his car and drove off in a belch of blue smoke.

Miss Eaton reconsidered: Wilfred and Joyce? Hilda wouldn't stand for that, and she controlled the purse that paid for Wilfred's painting. If Bullard had found out and put pressure on . . . yes, that would be a motive for murder.

She opened the newspaper to see that

Gray had done her proud. She had the front page headline:

PRIVATE EYE PROBES MURDER MYSTERY!

'Miss Isabel Eaton, top London investigator, has been hired to uncover the murderer at Porthcove Studios.

'After the police enquiry stalled, our reporter interviewed ace private eye Eaton, cigarette dangling from her lip. Miss Eaton, speaking in a tough American accent, stated firmly: 'I'll nail the killer before the cops do!'

'She promised *Herald* readers . . . '

Inspector Reid, coming out of the porch, paused as his eye caught the headline. He snatched at the paper, scanned it and snorted.

'Stupid rubbish. I'll can that reporter — and you, if you get in my way.'

He went quickly to his Rover and drove off. Miss Eaton was amused. He seemed quite upset.

She followed the path beside the annexe to the vegetable garden behind the studio, and saw Reggie Courtney talking to Bert. How easy it was to overlook Val's husband, she reflected. He stayed in the background, quietly getting on with his chores. It occurred to her that anyone so easily overlooked stood the best chance of seeing or hearing without being noticed.

She waited patiently till he had finished talking to the part-time gardener then, as he returned to the house, she intercepted him.

'What can you tell me about Joyce?' she asked.

'Joyce?' Reggie stared at her. 'She's a good cook. Reliable. Surely, you can't seriously suspect her?'

'I mean her background. Local girl? Married?'

'Joyce is local, yes. A widow actually. Her husband was a fisherman who was drowned in a storm. After that she applied for a job here.'

'And she never married again? Was there anyone before she married?'

Reggie shrugged. 'She never married again,' he agreed. 'Before? I wouldn't know — we haven't been here that long. Even after twelve years, we're still foreigners to Cornish people.'

'A pity. How did you get into this business anyway? It seems a bit unlikely for Val.'

'Val's a good organizer. She could run any kind of business. The chance of buying this studio came up — and we were fed up with city life, the dirt and the noise and petrol fumes.

'At the time I was working in an art-shop as a picture framer — I've always been good with my hands. That's where I met Keith. This place was advertised and we came down one weekend to look at it, liked Porthcove, and snapped it up.

'It's taken time and a lot of effort to build up the business. In fact, it's still a bit dodgy — but Keith put some money in to help out. So, providing we can live with this murder, we'll survive.'

'I suppose you get down to the harbour a fair bit?' Miss Eaton asked. 'A drink at the Inn?'

Reggie laughed. 'There's not much chance of that in the season. We don't have a big staff, as you've seen, so we do a lot of the work ourselves. In winter, yes

— we'll walk down for a quiet drink when the weather's good.'

And be on the spot for smuggling, Miss Eaton thought, and said, 'I imagine the winters can be bad on this coast. Did you notice anything special about George Bullard? Did he, for instance, speak to one person more than anyone else?'

'Not that I noticed — but then he seemed to spread his favours around.' Reggie grinned suddenly. 'Not that I had much to do with him — I took good care to avoid him. I just keep in the background mostly, doing the odd jobs. There's always enough of those to keep me busy.'

'The afternoon before Bullard died,' Miss Eaton probed. 'Bert seems sure he was here in the grounds. Keith confirms that.'

'Well, Bert would know.' Reggie paused. 'I was down at the harbour, buying fish.'

Miss Eaton noticed Constable Trewin approaching. Reggie said, 'I'm off. More to do than answer questions, you know.'

Miss Eaton watched him move away and vanish into a greenhouse. She gave her attention to the young constable, and decided he was looking down in the mouth.

'On your own now?' she asked lightly.

The local detective nodded.

'And it looks as though I'm being set up as the scapegoat if we don't catch this murderer. The Inspector's just informed me he's away to investigate a burglary — leaving me in charge here.'

'What's he like to work with?'

'All right, I suppose,' Trewin admitted grudgingly. 'For a foreigner. An old hand at looking after himself, I'd say. He only arrived from London a few months ago, chucking his weight about, and house-hunting for when he retires. That's the reason he put in for a transfer. He's sitting pretty, and doesn't intend to be involved in an investigation that doesn't lead to an arrest.'

'No leads then?'

Trewin shook his head.

'Too many people had a grudge against the dead man — and not only here. It could be anyone of them and, so far, there's no evidence pointing to one rather than another.'

He looked thoughtfully at Miss Eaton. 'I ought to warn you off, poking your nose into a murder enquiry, but . . . have you learnt anything?'

Miss Eaton smiled. Sherry strolled up, rubbed herself up against Constable Trewin's leg and purred loudly.

'She likes you . . . I've got one thing you might be interested in. Can we deal? You'll get the credit for any arrest of course — I'm only interested in seeing Val in the clear.'

Trewin hesitated, and made a fuss of her cat.

'Co-operate with a private 'tec? It's your duty to report anything you learn. Anyway, how do I know you won't blab to the papers? You seem well in with the local rag.'

'It was Gray who provided the lead.'

Trewin swore. 'Sorry.'

'I've heard worse,' Miss Eaton said. 'I'm a confidential enquiry agent. My living depends on keeping my mouth shut. Think about this — most people don't enjoy police questioning. But I'm on the inside. I can watch the suspects, while you have access to official information. Working together, we might come up with something.'

Trewin deliberated, then sighed and nodded.

'All right,' he agreed. 'We checked you out naturally, and you're clean. So we'll co-operate — but if you give anything to the press before I'm ready, I'll see you get done for it. Now, tell me what you know.'

'You first,' Miss Eaton said calmly.

He still hesitated before taking the plunge.

'Our enquiries show several possibilities. Dickson now, he's got a history of violence. He was running with a motorcycle gang and got involved in a fight. One of the rival gang had his head split open — it was only luck there wasn't a murder charge. Dickson got six months.

'Nicholas, the alleged psychic — she's known. Been up before the beak charged with fortune telling. One of her clients committed suicide after she gave a reading. She got away with a warning because the jury decided the victim's mind had been unbalanced before she gave the reading. The judge slammed into her all the same.'

'How terrible for her,' Miss Eaton murmured.

Trewin continued, 'Jacobi owns a small jewellers shop in a back street and is suspected of being a fence. He's sharp, and nothing's ever been proved against him, but his local bobby keeps an eye on him. The story is he deals in stolen property, furs and jewels and watches.'

'And if Bullard knew . . . I wonder why his body was left where it was? It would have been easy enough to drop it over the cliff into the sea.'

'We've considered that,' Trewin admitted, 'and we think the killer must have been disturbed and was too scared to go back.'

'So who disturbed him — or her?'

'Mr. Fletcher likes his booze, and he was at the Inn that night. I hear he'd had a skinful by the time he got back here — and that would be about the time of the murder. So he may have disturbed the murderer — if he didn't do it himself. We're checking with the Australian police to see if he's got a record, but that kind of long-distance enquiry takes time.'

Miss Eaton said, 'Or it may have been Duke and Linda coming back from the roadhouse.'

'Possibly,' Trewin agreed. 'At our interview, Jacobi seemed keen to throw suspicion on Mrs. Keller. After all, she discovered the body.'

'Convenient.'

'And Nicholas was adamant she wasn't going to help us in any way.'

'Silly, of course. Anything on Bullard yet?'

'Nothing criminal. We're looking to see if there's any hint of blackmailing in his past — but nothing so far. Now it's your turn.'

'This is what I got from Gray. Wilfred Keller is a local man and Joyce — the cook — is an old flame. There are possibilities there, I think.'

Trewin deliberated. 'Yes. His wife wouldn't like that. But it depends on Bullard knowing.'

'It's possible he was snooping around the house the previous afternoon and saw them together.'

Sherry began to miaow and Miss Eaton picked her up and stroked her.

'She does like people to make a fuss of her. It's not time for lunch yet — but perhaps a small sherry. Will you join me — er — constable?'

'Frank,' he said, and grinned. 'And frankly, I don't mind if I do!'

He had rather an engaging grin, Miss Eaton thought. But as they entered the house, Val Courtney called out:

'Telephone call for you, constable. It's the Inspector — and he says it's urgent.'

13

News from Birmingham

Detective Inspector Reid was feeling happy as he drove up to the front porch of the studio and got out of his Rover.

Trewin, alerted by his phone call, was waiting for him. 'The bike's around the side, sir. Dickson's in his room.'

'Get him.'

Reid walked to the car park to look at the Kawasaki 750 leaning against the wall. He bent over to study the pattern of the tyre treads, and grunted his satisfaction.

Trewin returned with Duke Dickson, who looked fed up.

'What's all this about then?' Duke asked angrily. 'First someone borrows my bike. Now — '

Reid smiled broadly. 'Got your story all ready, have you? It had better be good, lad.'

'I don't know what you're on about.'

'Arrange transport, constable,' Reid said briskly. 'I want this bike taken to the lab.'

'Do the tyres match?'

'As far as I can tell by looking, yes. It's up to the experts to prove it.'

Reid began to fill his pipe. 'Now, Mr. Dickson — did you go out on your bike last night? Or in the early hours of this morning?'

'No way are you going to pin anything on me. I was with Linda all the time.'

'As an alibi, I don't think your girlfriend will make a good showing in court.'

'Why would I need an alibi?'

'Because there was a break-in at Red Wheal last night. A valuable painting was stolen — worth several thousand pounds according to the owner. Tyre marks of a motorcycle are clearly visible in the grounds — marks that match the tyres on your machine.'

'Hell, there are plenty of bikes around with the same make of tyres. As far as I know, Kawasaki always fit Avon tyres.'

Reid shook his head, lit his pipe and said: 'We'll let the lab decide. Tyres wear differently, lad — I think we'll get a match.'

Duke flushed. 'You're just trying to frame me,' he said bitterly.

'We don't do that sort of thing. I'm asking you to accompany me to the station to help with enquiries. Are you coming quietly?'

Trewin tensed.

For a moment, Duke stood with clenched hands. He looked wildly about him as if he might lash out or make a run for it. Then his shoulders slumped.

Reid puffed contentedly on his pipe.

★　★　★

Miss Eaton overheard the end of their conversation as she hurried towards the car park.

'It's quite true, Inspector,' she said. 'Mr. Dickson mentioned this morning that someone had borrowed his machine.'

Reid gave her a long-suffering look. 'Well, he would, wouldn't he?'

She turned to Duke.

'I think you'd better go along with the Inspector, Duke. It's a formality, and nothing to worry about. I'll tell Linda where you are. You'll do no good by running away. The police will discover quickly enough that you're innocent and release you. It might not even be your bike that's involved.'

Duke Dickson looked beaten.

'I suppose I can't get out of it. I've been framed, that's what.'

'If you have, I'll do my best to find out who framed you.' Miss Eaton promised. He got into Reid's car and she watched them drive away. She thought: first a murder, and now a burglary — could there be a connection? Who could have used Duke's motorcycle last night?

A police van arrived in answer to Trewin's phone call and the Kawasaki was loaded aboard.

Miss Eaton returned to her room, stretched out on the bed and read a chapter of *Model For Murder*.

I was mad as two sidewinders with one rattle as I pistol-whipped the Man.

'Take me for a sucker, do you?' I screamed at him.

Bone crunched. Blood streaked his face. Teeth sprayed like gravel from a getaway car.

'First it looked like somebody framed Velma. Then it looked like somebody framed Josie.'

He was choking like he couldn't stand the taste of his own blood.

'It didn't work, wise guy. When I turned the notion around, I saw that somebody was just trying to take suspicion away from himself.'

The Man was tough as butter in a heat-wave when I'd finished beating a confession out of him . . .

It could be, Miss Eaton thought. But who was trying so hard to divert suspicion from himself?

When she looked at her bedside clock, she realized the painters would shortly be returning for dinner. She went outside and waited on the lawn.

Linda and Margo Nicholas carne up the hill carrying their sketching gear.

Miss Eaton said, 'Now, Linda, I don't

want you to start worrying, you — '

Linda turned pale. 'It's Duke, isn't it? What's happened to him? Is he hurt?'

She really does care about that young man, Miss Eaton thought, and beamed her approval. She always enjoyed a romance.

'The police have invited him to the station to answer some question, that's all. Apparently there was a burglary last night — '

'A burglary?' Linda seemed relieved by this idea. 'It's not the murder then?'

'Certainly not. A valuable painting has been stolen from a house not for away. The police believe that Duke's bike was used by the thief.'

'Well, someone did borrow it.'

'We know that,' Margo said. 'So obviously, there's no need to worry.'

'He was with me all night,' Linda said earnestly. 'I'll swear to it.'

'No doubt you went to sleep at some time,' Miss Eaton pointed out dryly.

'I'm a very light sleeper — the least thing disturbs me. But will they believe him?' The blonde girl seemed determined to worry. 'He's innocent, I know he is. He turned over a new leaf when we took the decision to live together. You're a detective — can you help? Find out who borrowed Duke's bike, I mean.'

'I'll help if I can,' Miss Eaton said.

'It's ridiculous, really. Why should Duke take a picture? He wouldn't know if it was worth anything — he knows even less about painting than I do.'

'And that's our thought for today,' Margo Nicholas said cheerfully. 'Hang on to it, Linda. Come on, I'll get you a drink before dinner.'

As they went into the house, Val called, 'Telephone for you, Belle.'

Miss Eaton picked up the receiver and put on her American accent: 'Eaton Investigations.'

Geary chuckled. 'Don't get tough with me, Isabel. You don't want to frighten me half to death, do you?' He became serious.

'First of all, it's going to be difficult to find anyone who'll grieve over Bullard's decease. Seems he was disliked by everyone he came in contact with

— apparently he made a life-long habit of upsetting people. That broadens the field quite a bit, I'd say.'

'I'll let the police worry about that.'

'Smart girl. As far as I can find out, no one benefits to any great extent. His wife divorced him years ago. There are no children or close relatives. He lived up to the hilt of his income. Just casual girlfriends — one night stands you might say.'

'I doubt it, Mr. Geary.'

'He worked as a valuer for several of the large insurance companies in Birmingham and was highly regarded in the profession. He specialized in valuing paintings and I'm told he had a sharp eye for a forgery.'

'How very interesting,' Miss Eaton said. 'That might be the lead I want. Can you find out one more thing for me please? If he ever valued any paintings for somebody named Jarvis at a place called Red Wheal?'

'Never satisfied, are you?' Geary's voice sounded cheerful. 'What's a red wheel when it's out?'

'The name of a house near Porthcove — there's been a painting stolen. And it's Wheal. Spelt W-H-E-A-L. Cornish for a mine.'

'Learning the lingo, are you?' Geary said. 'Okay, I'll get back to you. How's the murder business?'

'Quiet.'

Miss Eaton was thoughtful as she replaced the receiver. She had another idea. Perhaps it wasn't gems being smuggled into the country — but art treasures being taken out.

She had no doubt that a valuable painting could be sold to a private collector abroad. And Bullard had been connected with the insurance of paintings — an ideal set-up for a gang of art thieves.

And a motive for murder if the gang fell out.

She went in to dinner, which was a subdued affair.

'They're at it again,' Sammy said gloomily. 'The police are back, searching the place room by room — looking for the stolen painting I suppose.'

'They must be daft,' Margo declared in a ringing tone. 'If Duke took it — and I don't believe he did for one moment — he wouldn't bring it here.'

'You bet he wouldn't,' Fletcher added. 'No one in his right mind would. But you can't tell coppers anything — that Reid is a know-all. Duke wouldn't have the first idea how to get rid of a painting like that. And whoever took it knew what he was doing. You, can bet your life it's on its way to wherever it's going.'

'Where's that?' Margo asked.

Fletcher shrugged.

'A collector somewhere. You can be sure it had a new home — waiting before it was ever lifted. Maybe not even in this country.'

Miss Eaton kept a low profile. It occurred to her that the Australian sounded as if he knew something about dealing in stolen art treasures.

Linda Snow pushed back her plate, leaving the meal half-eaten.

'It's not fair,' she burst out, and hurried from the room.

After breakfast next morning, Miss

Eaton lingered over a second cup of coffee with Val. The telephone rang and Val hurried to answer it.

'For you, Belle.'

It was Geary, her Birmingham contact again.

'You're a good guesser,' he said. 'Bullard visited Red Wheal a few years back to value some paintings owned by Mr. Jarvis. The insurance company Bullard was representing at that time were reluctant to speak plainly, but admitted he recommended not insuring. Obviously he spotted something funny.'

'Thanks,' Miss Eaton said. 'I hope I can do as much for you one day.'

She got directions from Val and drove her small Fiat along narrow lanes that twisted between grey stone walls, up onto the moor. Red Wheal was sign-posted and, eventually, she came on an old tin mine. It was obviously shut down but the big winding wheel still stood at the minehead and, not far off, was the house of the mine owner.

She turned into a gravel drive that led to the front door. The house was weather-beaten and screened by a row of trees that hinted at the weather in winter on this exposed coast.

As she rang the bell, she recalled stories about wreckers and smugglers and highwaymen, and wondered if things had changed all that much. She looked back at the moor; even in sunlight it had a desolate air.

The door was opened by a servant.

'Eaton investigations,' she said crisply. 'Will you ask Mr. Jarvis if he can spare me a few minutes to discuss a matter of insurance.'

'I'll find out, Miss. If you'll wait in here.'

She was shown into a small room off the hall. There were brocaded chairs from a previous century, a grandfather clock, and Staffordshire pottery locked away behind glass.

Jarvis, when he appeared, was middle-aged with grey in his sideboards. He wore an expensive suit and his voice sounded pompous.

'If you're from an insurance company — '

Miss Eaton handed him her card. 'I'm a private investigator.'

'I see. Well, if you can recover my stolen Gauguin, I'll pay generously.'

'I believe Inspector Reid is looking into that.'

'I doubt if the police are concerned with getting my painting back. It struck me your Inspector was more concerned with making an arrest.'

Miss Eaton said, 'I'm investigating the murder of George Bullard. I've been told he visited here to value your paintings.'

'The man was a fool,' Jarvis said shortly. 'He refused to put a value on it — claimed the Gauguin was a fake. Ridiculous, of course — my own expert assured me it was genuine and I paid forty thousand for it.'

Miss Eaton refrained from comment. Instead, she asked, 'I assume the Gauguin was a part of your collection? Was only the one painting taken?'

'Yes, and yes.'

Jarvis produced a colour photograph of the painting. It showed peasants in a field; the forms were simplified, the colours flat

— more like a design for something, Miss Eaton thought.

'I want my picture back,' Jarvis said.

'How long is it since Bullard was here?'

'Oh, four, five years — something like that.'

'And that was the only time he visited?'

'I've never set eyes on him since. Didn't want to — an unpleasant man. Can't now, of course . . . '

14

Death of a Birdwatcher

Miss Eaton tapped lightly on the door of Keith Parry's room upstairs at the Porthcove Studios.

'Come.'

She opened the door and went in.

'Sorry to interrupt your rest, Keith,' she said. 'Val told me you were taking five after lunch.'

Parry was stretched out on top of his bed, shoes off and ankles crossed, his hands behind his head.

'I always relax when I can — helps to keep me on top-line, I find. I'll be going down to the harbour any minute now — so what can I do for Val's favourite private eye?'

Miss Eaton perched birdlike on the edge of a chair and handed him the photograph of Jarvis's stolen painting.

'What can you tell me about this?

There seems to be some doubt that it's a genuine Gauguin.'

Parry took the photograph and studied it for some moments.

'I'm not familiar with this painting,' he admitted. 'But that proves nothing. Not all pictures get reproduced in art books — especially if they're in private collections. I'd need to see the original to form an opinion.' He rose from the bed in a single graceful movement and took a book from the shelf. He turned the pages, pausing at different reproductions to compare with the photograph.

'I seem to remember seeing a film based on Gauguin's life,' Miss Eaton remarked.

Parry answered absently.

'Yes . . . based on Somerset Maugham's book, 'The Moon and Sixpence'. Fiction, of course . . . impossible to be sure from a photograph. It looks as though it might be genuine, but . . . ' He shrugged.

'I thought forgers only went in for old Masters,' Miss Eaton said brightly. 'Dutch artists — Van Meegeren painted some, I believe.'

'You're right about Van Meegeren, but wrong about the Old Masters. Plenty of modern artists are faked. It's something of a joke in the art world — there are more Picassos in museums and art galleries than he ever painted.'

Parry looked thoughtfully at her. 'Can I take it this is a photo of the stolen painting?'

'You can.'

'But if, as you appear to think, this is a forgery, why would anyone steal it?'

'So perhaps it isn't.' Miss Eaton shrugged. 'Or perhaps the thief believed it was genuine. Jarvis certainly does.'

'Confusing,' Parry said, and laughed.

'Isn't it?'

They went downstairs together. Keith Parry whistled as he walked towards the road leading down to the harbour.

Miss Eaton brought a chair from the hall and sat in the sunshine on the lawn. She sat where Bert had told her Bullard set up his easel on the last afternoon of his life. She looked at the roses he had painted but no inspiration came.

She thought about the stolen picture

that George Bullard had declared a forgery. Suppose he had been wrong? Even an expert can be wrong occasionally.

Or suppose he'd been lying? If the painting weren't insured, would the police investigate as thoroughly? Possibly not.

So a valuable painting could be smuggled out of the country . . . and Bullard was dead. A gang of art thieves, a double-cross and murder. And then the theft?

The sequence seemed wrong. She felt irritated and sighed and closed her eyes.

Trewin's voice aroused her.

'It's all right for some. You don't have an Inspector chasing you for a report.'

Miss Eaton opened her eyes. 'What's the news about Duke?'

'Reid's still holding him. The lab is sure it's his bike involved.'

'There's a French boat in harbour, the Jean Michel — '

Trewin grinned. 'Reid may be a pain, but he isn't daft. He got Customs to board and search her — no painting.'

'Bullard was at Red Wheal before,' Miss Eaton said.

197

'Was he now? That's intcresting. D'you think there's a link between his murder and the robbery? No, that's wrong — he was killed first.'

'There has to be a link, Frank,' Miss Eaton said.

'Not necessarily — coincidences do happen.' Trewin looked across the lawn to the house. 'I'm off to the inn. Be my guest. You can't visit Cornwall and not sample our local mead.'

★　★　★

Margo Nicholas had found the shade of some rocks. She sat on her stool, sketchpad on her lap, engrossed in drawing the steps cut into the cliff face. She thought she had something good.

Parry joined her on his round of the students.

'Interesting, Margo. You're the first this time to see the steps as a subject. Usually someone gets around to them during the fortnight. Let me sit there, will you?'

She rose and Parry took her place, looking from her pad to the cliff steps.

'I like your attack. Nice and bold, but with this particular subject, correct drawing is essential. And your perspective isn't quite right.'

He turned a page and made a quick sketch.

'Like that — d' you see? What I suggest is, make an accurate drawing first, then work it up afterwards. Okay?'

'I suppose so.' Margo sighed. 'Drawing was never my strong point.'

Parry smiled briefly. 'All the more reason to work at it then.'

Margo shielded her eyes from the glare of the sun and looked up at the top of the flight of stone steps.

'Isn't that Mrs. Keller up there? She's got her binoculars on us.'

Parry glanced at his watch. 'More likely checking on Wilfred — she's a very possessive woman. I'm popping up to the tearooms for a break. Care to join me?'

'Not now. I want to get this drawing right.'

'That's the idea. See you at dinner.'

Margo watched him lope away with long-legged strides towards the harbour and the road leading up the hill. She turned to a new sheet in her pad and sighed as she prepared to start a new sketch.

She glanced up at Mrs. Keller, put out her tongue and bent her head over her pad.

Hilda Keller squatted awkwardly on the topmost ledge of the steps cut into the cliff face. A wide-brimmed hat shielded her eyes from the sun as she scanned the bay through her binoculars.

She could see Margo Nicholas below, alone, seated on a stool, sketching.

She had seen Linda earlier, from her vantage point by the tea-rooms. The blonde girl hadn't been painting, just sitting and throwing stones in the water. Brooding. Hilda thought, pining for her boyfriend. A foolish girl; she was well rid of him.

The jew and that nice Australian had been further along the quay, painting side by side. And where, she wondered, was Wilfred?

It occurred to her that her post outside the tea-rooms was getting well-known, and she shifted to the top of the steps. Gulls wheeled and dived about the cliffs, screeching.

Was Margo waiting for Wilfred? Could he really be interested in that gypsy-looking woman with her ridiculous ear-rings?

And if he did turn up, could she get down the steps in time to confront them? She doubted it. The steps were narrow and looked dangerous.

She watched the tutor come along the sand and stop to give Margo instruction. He walked quickly back towards the harbour.

Margo went on sketching and Hilda waited. Eventually Margo gave up and looked up at her; she folded her stool and carried her sketching gear back towards the harbour.

Hilda watched till she was out of sight. There was still no sign of Wilfred. She wondered if Margo had gone to meet him and decided she would return to the tea-rooms.

She started to get to her feet, but she was sitting awkwardly and moved slowly.

She felt a pair of hands at the small of her back. She turned her head and said, 'Is that you, Wilfred?'

The hands pushed hard and she toppled outwards, losing her balance. She made a wild grab for the rock face but her hands closed about air.

'Wilfred!' she screamed as she fell.

Her scream was lost in the screeching of the gulls and the noise of water breaking over rocks.

* * *

Miss Eaton decided that mead was not to her taste. Used to a dry sherry, she found the honey drink too sweet for her palate.

Her session at the Harbour Inn ended when Trewin was called to the telephone.

Walking back up the hill on her own, she felt drowsy. Alcohol and heat, she thought, adds up to an afternoon nap. She was not expecting any immediate developments, so there was no reason why she shouldn't indulge herself.

She found a gap in the hedge and

squeezed through. She found a patch of soft grass and stretched out in the sun. Nice, she thought sleepily . . .

She woke with a start, yawning, and glanced at her watch. The afternoon had vanished; if she didn't hurry, she'd be late for dinner.

She walked briskly up the hill to her room, splashed cold water over her face and went along to the dining room. Dinner had just started and everyone appeared subdued.

'What's happened?' she asked.

Sammy said, 'Mrs. Keller is dead. She fell from the top of the cliff steps — '

'I was sketching at the bottom of the steps.' Margo's face was unusually pale. 'I saw her up top, using her binoculars. Then I finished my drawing and left. It must have happened soon afterwards.' She drew a deep breath. 'I'm glad it didn't happen before I'd left, that's all.'

Fletcher said grimly, 'So, did she fall — or was she pushed? The cops have taken Wilfred to the station.' He mimicked an English accent: 'To help with our enquiries. And we all know what that means.'

'If it was murder, we can guess why, can't we?' Sammy said. 'She was always spying through her binoculars. A joke, really, her keeping an eye on Wilfred, but she must have seen everything that goes on around here. She must have spotted something someone wanted to keep quiet.'

'Well,' Miss Eaton said. 'We'll never know now, will we?'

She ate quietly, wondering what it could have been that Mrs. Keller saw.

When Joyce brought in the dessert, she looked upset. Did she suspect her lover of killing his wife?

Miss Eaton made a smile for Linda. 'I should imagine the police will be releasing Duke soon,' she said brightly.

'I hope so.'

When she had finished her meal, Miss Eaton strolled into the kitchen. Sherry, well-fed and content, had rolled onto her back, inviting the cook to play with her. She seemed hurt that Joyce should ignore her.

Miss Eaton rubbed the Persian's stomach till she purred.

'Is it true they've arrested Mr. Keller?' Joyce asked nervously.

'I don't think they've arrested him. But it's usual to question the husband of a woman who dies in suspicious circumstances.'

'Wilfred wouldn't have pushed her,' Joyce muttered. 'He's not like that.'

'You know him well?'

'I suppose it's bound to come out now. He was visiting me when he could get away. It was just a bit of fun.'

Miss Eaton didn't think it had been just a bit of fun for Joyce.

'She kept him you know. All he was interested in was his painting. He was always like that.' The cook seemed sad.

Miss Eaton said: 'I think you should be told that the local reporter knows you were friendly with Wilfred before you married.'

'Does it matter?'

'It might. The police, suspicious by the nature of their job, might think you pushed her.'

'Oh, I never would!' Joyce looked shocked.

Miss Eaton thought she was probably telling the truth and urged Sherry out into the garden.

The blue Persian was in a playful mood and made straight for Reggie as he used a hose to water the dry earth. She sneaked up behind him and rubbed herself against the back of his legs.

'Made me jump,' he said.

Sherry was purring.

'She knows who likes her,' Miss Eaton said, and thought: what's he scared of?

Reggie Courtney kept darting nervous glances about the garden. 'How's the investigation going? Any ideas yet?'

'I've one or two ideas. Obtaining proof is the problem.'

Reggie was sweating badly. He wiped his face with a handkerchief.

'I don't know what's going on here,' he muttered. 'First Bullard — now the Keller woman. I suppose she was pushed? Everyone seems to assume so. That would make a second murder — any more and we'll have to shut down.'

'Do you know any reason why there should be more?'

'Of course not. What d'you mean?'

'Do you suspect someone in particular?'

Reggie didn't answer. He looked towards the house, his head cocked to one side.

'That's Val calling . . . must go.'

Miss Eaton gazed after him. She hadn't heard anyone call and her hearing was good.

She walked through the gardens towards the front of the house, leaving Sherry chasing butterflies.

Constable Trewin came up the hill from the Inn, his ginger hair flaming in the evening sun.

'What's new?' Miss Eaton asked.

'We've got a line on Fletcher. The Australian police have suspicions — no proof, no convictions — that he's a con-man.'

Miss Eaton nodded. 'He's a good talker, popular.'

'He certainly smooth-talked Mrs. Keller and she held the purse-strings. If Bullard had suspicions too, he wasn't the sort to keep his mouth shut. A strong motive for murder if Fletcher's pulling a con here. Now Wilfred gets her money and I've got to question Mrs. Willis.'

Trewin paused. 'Reid thinks it's murder — '

'I'm inclined to agree.'

' — and he's blaming me. I'm investigating one murder when there's a second.'

'That's ridiculous. You weren't to know, and you can't be everywhere. He might as well blame me because I took an afternoon nap.'

'He probably will,' Trewin said. 'And nobody will have an alibi. They'll be scattered all over the landscape, painting. Anyone of 'em could have done it.'

'Joyce is upset already,' Miss Eaton warned. 'It might be a good idea if I'm with you when you question her.'

Trewin hesitated, then nodded. 'Why not?'

When they entered the kitchen, Joyce was cleaning down her workbench.

'Mrs. Willis,' Trewin said, 'I have to ask you where you were at approximately four o'clock this afternoon.'

Joyce answered reluctantly.

'I was out walking, alone. When anything worries me, I always walk it off.'

'I know what you mean,' Miss Eaton said sympathetically.

'I was upset about the murder of Mr. Bullard and the police being here asking questions. I thought they might start asking about me and Wilfred.'

'Did you walk along the cliff path?' Trewin probed.

'No. I went inland, away from the coast. I was worried in case his wife got to hear about us — or see us together.'

'So you pushed her over the cliff?'

'No, no . . . '

'Was Wilfred Keller with you?'

Joyce looked to Miss Eaton for help.

'Only the truth will help Wilfred.'

'I didn't see him at all today.'

'Did you see anyone?' Trewin asked. 'Did anyone see you?'

Joyce shook hor head dumbly. She seemed to be about to burst into tears.

'What's going to happen to Wilfred?' she wailed.

★　★　★

Margo Nicholas sat on the edge of her bed, smoking a last cigarette. Perhaps he was shy? She liked Sammy Jacobi; they seemed to suit each other and she was definitely interested.

She thought he was interested too and she could usually tell. So it annoyed her that he didn't make any move in her direction. Should she make the first move? Or would that put him right off?

Some men, she knew, resented being pursued by a woman. Well, this holiday wasn't going to last for ever, and she could always make the excuse that she felt nervous — which was true enough. Just thinking about Hilda Keller hurtling down the cliff steps made her shiver.

She made up her mind, adjusted her dressing gown and stubbed out her cigarette. She switched off the light and listened at the door. No one was moving about and it was quiet except for Jim Fletcher snoring.

She opened the door and noved silently along the darkened corridor to Sammy's room. She held her breath as she passed Miss Eaton's room, shuddered at the thought of George Bullard's empty room.

She eased open the door and slid inside, closing it behind her.

The room was still and dark.

'It's me, Margo,' she whispered. 'Sammy?'

There was no answer.

Her eyes became accustomed to the gloom. She felt suddenly foolish when she realised she was talking to an empty room.

15

View from the Cliff

Miss Eaton made sure that all the students were down by the harbour before she walked along the cliff path, carrying her binoculars and accompanied by Sherry.

The sky was still cloudless but the morning sun had not yet reachod its full heat.

She reached the top of the steps, which had been roped off and a warning posted: *Danger*. The police, after searching the area, had left.

She looked carefully behind her, having no wish to join Hilda Keller in a death fall, but she was alone as far as she could see.

She stepped over the rope and warily approached the flight of steps leading down to the bay. She moved down three steps so she could be out of sight and left

Sherry sitting on the top step. The blue Persian could be counted on to warn her if anyone approached.

Miss Eaton shaded her binoculars with one hand and focussed them. The late Mrs. Keller had a good eye for a vantage point. From the steps she had a clear view of the headland and fishing boats putting out to sea. One of them, she noted, was the *Jean Michel*.

None of the holiday painters had ventured along the shore; they were huddled together near the harbour.

She saw nothing out of the ordinary, and she began to doubt that Hilda had seen anything that made her a risk to Bullard's murderer. Slowly she moved her head, studying the shoreline inch by inch.

The water was calm, its surface unruffled except where it met rocks. Sunlight glinted on a sea as clear as glass. She saw jagged edges of rock and clumps of weed below the surface. And something else.

Excitement pulsed through her. It was something that had no right to be where it was. She noted carefully the position of the object, put away her binoculars and climbed to the top of the steps.

What she needed now was a public call box. She wanted privacy for this phone call. She started to jog along the path towards the road, remembering she had seen a call box outside the souvenir shop in the village.

★ ★ ★

Dinner that evening was a subdued affair. Duke and Wilfred were still helping the police with their enquiries. It seemed to Miss Eaton that, for the first time, the seriousness of the situation was sinking in.

Before, they had been glad to see the last of George Bullard. But Hilda's death had shaken them.

They looked uneasily at each other, obviously wondering if the killer sat around the table and who it might be. And who the next victim might be.

Miss Eaton observed that Margo was barely on speaking terms with Sammy and speculated on the cause. Linda and

Joyce looked worried. Jim Fletcher appeared to be deep in thought.

At the small table, Val tried to catch her eye. Reggie looked down at his plate and ate in silence. Only Parry tried to keep a conversation going.

After dinner, Margo made a fuss of Sherry.

'I've got five cats of my own,' she said. 'Not pedigree animals like yours — just strays I've given a home to.' She waited till the others were out of hearing. 'I may be able to help.'

Miss Eaton murmured, 'It's a nice evening — let's walk in the garden.'

'Help to find the killer, I mean,' Margo said as they strolled around the goldfish pond. 'I'm a genuine psychic. If you can provide something of George's, I may be able to provide a clue. From the psychic aura.'

Miss Eaton looked at her enquiringly.

'It's called psychometry. By holding a personal object in my hand, I can receive extra-sensory perceptions that tell me about the people and circumstances connected with that object.'

Miss Eaton said, 'I imagine the police have all of Bullard's personal effects under lock and key. And I doubt if I could persuade Inspector Reid to go along with your object reading.'

Margo scowled. 'You can bet the Inspector won't — he doesn't like me at all.'

'Yes, I heard that one of your clients died. I'm sorry.'

Margo looked unhappy. 'It's always being dug up and thrown at me. I was younger then, and used to speak my mind. It taught me a lesson. I'm careful now to temper any bad news . . . but if you can somehow get hold of something personal of George's, I can try. It might give you a lead.'

'I'll keep that in mind,' Miss Eaton said.

'You must find this murderer and clear the rest of us. I shan't feel safe until he's arrested and put in prison.'

As Margo Nicholas left her, Miss Eaton wondered: was it a genuine offer, or something else? And, if genuine, could she really do anything?

She thought Trewin might be persuaded to get hold of something of Bullard's. Failing that, Wilfred might loan some personal item belonging to Hilda . . . it was an idea.

Miss Eaton rose early the next morning and went for her regular training run. If anyone had their eye on her, it wouldn't appear she was breaking her usual routine. A watcher would not be aware that under her jogging suit she wore a bathing costume.

She turned out of the drive and ran down the hill to the harbour. The sky was light by the time she reached the quay and found Constable Trewin waiting in a dinghy.

She jumped aboard and he unloosed the rope and pushed off.

'What's this all about?'

'Wait and see.'

Trewin used the oars skilfully, the blades barely skimming the water's surface on their return.

Outside the harbour, Miss Eaton instructed, 'Keep well inshore. I don't want anybody up at the studio to see us.'

'So that's why you specified no engine on the phone.'

She nodded. 'Aim for the cliff steps.'

Trewin rowed easily and Miss Eaton watched the shore and calculated the spot she wanted.

'It looks different down here.' She drew a mental line from the steps to the rocks. 'About there, I think.' She pointed.

The water remained calm, gently lapping at projecting crags of rock as the dinghy edged between them.

She peered down. Everything looked distorted, a jumble of odd shapes formed from rock and seaweed.

'About here will do. I hope.'

Miss Eaton shed her tracksuit and went over the side in a clean dive. Down and down, holding her breath and feeling the cold bite. She clung to a rock, trying not to disturb the water. It was difficult to see — a sandy bottom, some shells and a starfish. And, yes, there it was — an oblong shape.

She swam towards it and tried to lift it. The thing was heavy and resisted her effort to raise it. Then she saw the cord around it.

She swam back up to the dinghy and held on to the side till she got her breath back.

'It's weighted. Have you got a knife, Frank?'

Trewin took a clasp knife from his pocket, opened it and handed it to her handle first.

She sucked air into her lungs and dived again, this time straight onto the object. She sawed away at the cord. It was tough — nylon probably — and not easy to cut underwater.

She went up again and rested, breathing deeply.

'Nearly got it. This time.'

She dived a third time, slashed through the frayed cord, releasing the canvas from its iron weight and brought it up with her.

She handed it to Trewin and climbed into the boat. He handed her a towel and she dried herself and put on her tracksuit.

'Well,' Trewin said admiringly. 'You've found Jarvis's stolen picture for the Inspector. And he's just going to love you for showing him up — but why would anyone chuck it into the sea?'

'I've got ideas about that,' Miss Eaton said, and took the oars. She needed the exercise to warm her up.

'Listen Frank, you hand the Gauguin to Reid and let him return it.' What am I saying? she thought. Jarvis offered to pay me to get it back. What I do for St. Agatha's! 'That'll keep him out of our way.'

'And wrap it in the towel when you go ashore. I want to get back to the studio before anybody realises I've been swimming. That would spoil everything.'

'Yes? Have you got any more ideas? The holiday painters will be going home this weekend, and I'm damn sure one of them is the murderer. We can't hold them all on suspicion. They'll be spread right across the country, and Reid will see I get the blame for not catching the murderer.'

Miss Eaton smiled.

'Stop worrying, Frank — I've got an idea to persuade the killer to give himself away. So let the Inspector grab the credit for getting Jarvis's picture back. You'll have your murderer!'

16

Return of the Prodigals

After lunch, Miss Eaton waited until the annexe was deserted, then went on the prowl. First she entered Margo's room and took a long hard look at her cheap jewellery. Dissatisfied, she searched Sammy's room.

As an afterthought, she went through Fletcher's room without finding anything incriminating. Not that she expected to.

She decided she had too many ideas on the boil, any one of which might be the right one. Or two. She returned to her room, opened the window wide — the afternoon was hot, dry and windless — and stretched out on the bed.

She felt drowsy and her subconscious recalled a Sam Pike story, *The Medium Screams Murder*:

The room had wallpaper the colour of blood and smelled of incense.

Doctor Origami, lost in a striped bathrobe, sat across the table from me. A single ruby gleamed in his turban, like an evil third eye.

He hunched over a crystal ball and his voice hissed like a snake about to strike.

'I see death, Mr, Pike . . . your death!'

But I was already moving. The blade of a throwing knife drew a bead of blood from my ear in passing.

'You cheap blackmailer,' I snarled, and crowned him with his own crystal ball . . .

Suddenly Miss Eaton wasn't sleepy any more. She felt sure her idea was going to work.

★   ★   ★

Val Courtney said, 'Have you any news for me, Belle?'

Miss Eaton was in the upstairs sitting room, enjoying a sherry before dinner.

'Soon now,' she murmured absently. 'Things are coming to a head.'

She heard a car drive up and left her chair to look out of the window. It was a police car, and Duke Dickson and Wilfred Keller got out. The car drove away.

Val joined her at the window. 'You don't seem surprised, Belle.'

'The police have no real evidence to make a charge stick.'

She watched Linda run out of the house, throw her arms around Duke and kiss him. Then Fletcher, smiling broadly, came up to Wilfred and took his arm.

'Wilf, mate, I'm sorry about Hilda. Look, you don't want to stay at the inn on your own. Bunk in with me for tonight — we'll get sloshed together. How about it?'

Wilfred looked grateful. 'I think I'd like that,' he said.

Miss Eaton frowned, finished her sherry and hurried downstairs. She intercepted them as they came into the hall.

'Mr. Fletcher. May I have a quiet word with you?'

'Why not? Excuse me a moment, Wilf.'

When they were alone, Miss Eaton said, 'The local police have heard from Australia, where you appear to be well

223

known. If I were you, I'd forget about exploiting Mr. Keller.'

Fletcher's face flushed angrily. 'You can't prove a thing. Open your mouth, and I'll sue!'

'Just remember the police have their eye on you.'

She turned, and hurried after Wilfred.

'Mr. Keller, I need your help. I believe I can expose your wife's murderer, and that will lift suspicion off you.'

His face brightened at once.

'I'll do anything. I can't — er — marry again while people think I killed Hilda. I didn't, you know.'

'I believe you,' Miss Eaton said. 'What I want is something personal of Hilda's. Some object that she handled every day.'

Keller looked surprised, then doubtful.

'It seems an odd request if I might say so. Will a hair-brush do?'

'Admirably . . . '

Miss Eaton was already moving away from him, through the common room and along the passage to Margo's room. She knocked on the door.

When it opened, she slipped inside and

closed the door. Margo had pans and a rag in her hand, obviously about to clean the ink off the tools she had been using. A sketch pad, showing a drawing of the customs house was propped up on the bedside table.

'I'm taking you up on that idea of yours for an object reading,' Miss Eaton said quickly. 'Wilfred will provide a hair-brush of Mrs. Keller's. Will you do it?'

'Of course I will,' Margo said. 'I can tell you, I'm more than a bit nervous with a murderer on the loose. There's no telling who he might pick on next. And when we leave here and go our separate ways, whoever it is could pick us off one by one. I'm convinced it's a maniac.'

'I don't think so,' Miss Eaton said confidently. 'And I'm sure I can remove any danger to you. Now listen carefully . . . '

She told Margo Nicholas exactly what she wanted her to do. As she passed through the common room to look for Keith Parry, she paused to look at the painting of fishing boats entering Porthcove harbour, and chided herself: I should have noticed that before. She moved on, shaking her head gently. It was true, she thought; what was right under your nose all the time was the one thing you never really saw.

She found the tutor with Val in the hall as she was locking the art shop door.

Miss Eaton said calmly, 'I'm planning to trap our murderer this evening. Keith, you can help if you will.'

'But it's our exhibition evening! We always have one before the course ends and I've just been fixing it with Val . . . but yes, I'll help, naturally. Just let me know what you want. Poor Reggie is worried stiff.'

'This needn't interfere with your exhibition. In fact, that may even be useful — it'll get everyone together.'

Miss Eaton turned to Val.

'Can you lay on some drinks and a snack afterwards? I want to keep people together while I try a little experiment.'

'Anything to settle this business,' Val Courtney said eagerly. 'I'll tell Reggie and Joyce. What are you going to do?'

Miss Eaton smiled, and went to make a

couple of phonecalls.

When Gray and Miss Eaton entered the studio, the holiday painters were already gathered there. Around the walls were pinned one sketch by each of the students, selected by their tutor for special comment.

'I hope you don't mind my inviting Mr. Gray,' she said. 'But I promised him a story.'

Keith Parry smiled. 'Welcome, Mr. Gray. Perhaps the 'Herald' will give Porthcove Studios a bit of publicity?'

Gray, breathing beer fumes, lit a cigarette and waved smoke into the air. 'I might just do that.'

Miss Eaton found two seats at the back and they sat down. She noticed that Parry's demonstration painting of the harbour was still on an easel — and Duke and Linda were holding hands.

The students looked a bit subdued. A public criticism was not the same thing as a word in private, she imagined. She watched faces as Parry began his commentary.

'I especially like this one of Margo's,

with the sea breaking over rocks. As an example of the use of mixed media, it's worth your study. Very nice, Margo.'

He moved next to an oil painting of The High Street.

'Jim, this is still a bit on the slick side. More like an illustration than a painting, in my opinion. It's good, but you need to loosen up — take a chance now and then.'

He paused before a water-colour of fishermen's cottages.

'Linda, I'm pleased with this effort — you're really beginning to make progress. The drawing of the houses isn't quite right — the left-hand wall looks as if it's falling over. You need a lot more practice at drawing. Don't rush to start painting — take your time and look hard. Don't ever forget, painting is seeing. As I've said before, water-colour is a difficult medium so, when you get home, try poster colours.

'Next, a pastel by Wilfred. Competent as usual. It would do no harm to try less conventional subjects — a coil of rope or a reflection in a puddle. Something you have to look at closely. This should help you to develop.'

He stopped in front of an oil impasto of fishing boats.

'Well, Sammy, you're certainly using your paint thicker. Quite a juicy effect here. But it needs more control, I feel. Again, the drawing could do with some attention — and I'd like to see you try for rather more subtle effects in the colour. Try a cerulean blue for the sky, for instance.

'That's about it. I hope you've enjoyed your painting, and that our two beginners will go on with it. Now — '

The door opened and Val Courtney came in, with Reggie and Joyce. She was pushing a kitchen trolley with plates of savouries, wine bottles and glasses.

'We're throwing a bit of a party,' she said, 'because your holiday has been spoilt.'

Reggie Courtney and Joyce got busy handing around glasses of wine and persuading people to help themselves. Gray needed no persuasion.

When they were all served and seated

again, Val said: 'And now Miss Eaton has something to say.'

Miss Eaton looked at Margo and Keith Parry, and nodded. Margo brandished a hairbrush, and Parry slipped out of the room.

17

Revelations

Miss Eaton dominated the room. She had a small table in front of her, and the holiday painters and residents of Porthcove Studios sat on chairs or stools grouped in a half-circle about her. Behind her was an easel supporting Parry's demonstration painting.

Some were still eating, others held wine glasses. Wilfred, she noticed, was chain-smoking.

From her handbag, Miss Eaton brought a pint bottle of Kentucky Bourbon and half filled a tumbler. She lit a Camel and let it dangle from her bottom lip. She placed her Smith and Wesson on the table, beside an old newspaper, a piece of rag and Trewin's clasp knife.

When she spoke, she used her tough American voice.

'Waal now, all the suspects are gathered

and tonight we are going to unmask a murderer. A double murderer. Some of you wanted to shield the person who killed George Bullard — but attitudes have changed since Hilda Keller was pushed to her death. You're not sure who might be next . . . '

She paused, and beckoned Margo to take the empty chair next to her.

'Margo Nicholas, a genuine psychic, has agreed to help. Margo . . . '

Margo held up the hair-brush, and said solemnly:

'This brush is the property of Mrs. Hilda Keller, deceased. What I am about to perform is called 'psychometry'. Some of you, perhaps, will be familiar with the term. For the benefit of the others, I shall explain.'

Miss Eaton leaned back in her chair, watching faces. Gray's cheroot had gone out and he chewed the end as he scribbled in his notebook.

'All personal objects handled daily gather some of the aura of the owner,' Margo said. 'A psychic can sense this aura — and sometimes get an accurate reading from the object. It can tell me something about the owner. In the case of violent death, I can receive a message from the departed. This may be a cry for vengeance. Sometimes the identity of a murderer may be revealed.'

Someone coughed. Feet shuffled.

'May I have quiet, please? I am going to try for a message from beyond, and I need absolute silence so that I can concentrate. No distractions, if you please.'

The room grew quiet. Gray scribbled furiously. Every eye was riveted on Margo Nicholas as she closed her eyes and took deep breaths.

Miss Eaton studied each face in turn. Linda clutched Duke's hand, her face pale. Reggie Courtney looked unhappy. Fletcher shifted uneasily.

Margo seemed to go into a trance and, when she spoke next, it was in a different voice. A disembodied voice.

'I see white mist . . . the mist clears slowly and I see the figure of a woman . . . she is sitting high up . . . now a pair of hands . . . behind her, a man!'

It seemed as if everyone drew a deep breath at the same time. Tension grew in the studio. The only sound was that of the strange voice coming from Margo's lips.

'The man moves stealthily . . . his hands reach out for the sitting figure . . . and pushes. As she falls, he says 'Schmuck'!'

The last word was spoken in an accurate imitation of Sammy Jacobi's voice.

Sammy leapt to his feet, his face flushed and hands gesturing wildly.

'It's a lie! A lie — I never killed anybody in my life. I swear it!'

On cue, Keith Parry entered the room and placed a box of oil paints on the table in front of Miss Eaton.

He said, 'From Sammy's room, as you instructed,' and took a seat.

Margo came out of her trance and asked, 'Did anything happen?'

Sammy looked as if he wanted to bolt, but daren't.

'Sit down, Mr. Jacobi,' Miss Eaton said sharply.

Reluctantly, he obeyed. Miss Eaton

opened the box of paints and took out several fat tubes of new oil colours. Jacobi watched apprehensively as she used Trewin's clasp knife to slit them open.

Red, blue and yellow oil paint oozed out onto the sheet of newspaper — and something else. Small, hard objects. She wiped one with a piece of rag till it shone and sparkled. A diamond.

'Stolen in Amsterdam,' she said briskly, 'and brought across in the *Jean Michel*.'

Reggie Courtney's eyes glazed over. He looks as if he couldn't believe his own eyes, Miss Eaton thought.

'All right,' Jacobi said, standing up. 'So I'm a fence — I admit it . . . But that doesn't mean I killed anyone. I swear I didn't.'

Margo Nicholas looked unhappy.

Miss Eaton tapped her Smith and Wesson to remind them who was in charge.

'Sit down!' She waited till he was seated again. 'But a strong motive, if Bullard had got onto you and exerted pressure. But there are others here with, perhaps, an equally strong motive for murder . . . '

★　★　★

Frank Trewin sat quietly on a chair behind the door in Miss Eaton's room in the annexe. The door was ajar so he had a view of the passage. He waited.

He'd come in from the garden, unobserved, while everyone was at dinner, obeying the instructions Miss Eaton had given over the 'phone.

Inspector Reid was at Red Wheal, no doubt basking in glory after returning the stolen Gauguin. Trewin doubted if Miss Eaton would get a mention. So, if she came up trumps again, he'd arrest the murderer himself.

She was good, no doubt about it. He felt mounting excitement and wondered what she had in mind.

Presently he heard footsteps. The door of the common room opened and Parry stepped into the corridor. Trewin held his breath and watched.

Parry went into Jacobi's room and came out carrying a box of oil paints. Just what Miss Eaton had told him would happen.

Parry went back through the common room and Trewin padded silently after him. The tutor waited outside the door of the studio.

Jacobi's voice came; 'Schmuck!'

Parry walked into the studio.

They're all there now, Trewin thought, set up for whatever surprise she's going to spring.

Quietly he sneaked up and opened the door a fraction. He heard Miss Eaton talking in her American voice.

'Mr. Keller, of course, was enjoying a liaison with Joyce — and would have lost a comfortable living if his wife had found out. Joyce hoped to marry Wilfred, I believe. Either of them has a strong motive for murder if Bullard had discovered them together — and don't forget that Hilda was also murdered.'

Joyce gave a little sob. 'I never did!'

Miss Eaton paused, took a sip from her glass of bourbon and lit a fresh cigarette. Sherry jumped onto her lap, sniffed at the glass and settled down.

'Then there are Val and Reggie Courtney. Val asked me to get rid of

Bullard for them — they were scared that his unpleasantness would lose them business. This motive applies to Mr. Parry. Not only did part of his income derive from this studio, but he had also put money of his own into the business.'

Parry grinned easily. 'I wish I'd thought of it,' he murmured. 'I'd have finished off George a lot earlier in the week.'

Miss Eaton ignored the interruption.

'There's Duke, with a police record of violence. He flared up quickly when Bullard made a pass at Linda. He might easily have lost control a second time. And Linda might have felt threatened when he asked her to pose in the nude — perhaps she was afraid it wouldn't stop at posing. Let's not forget she was the only visitor any good with a boomerang.'

Miss Eaton chain-lit another cigarette, coughed, and stubbed out the old butt. Gray scribbled in his notebook.

'Which brings us to the obvious suspect — Mr. Fletcher. An expert with both a boomerang and killing stick, the actual murder weapon. And suspected by the Australian police of being a conman — '

Wilfred gave a start.

' — a strong motive if he was planning to con money out of Mrs. Keller, and Bullard found out about him.'

'You can't prove anything,' Fletcher said angrily. 'Why should I kill Hilda, if you're right?'

'Someone killed them both,' Miss Eaton said. 'And for a good reason. But we mustn't forget our psychic, Margo Nicholson. Known to the police as a fortune-teller and in some trouble in the past when one of her clients took her own life. Perhaps Bullard knew about this and she didn't want it to come out here.'

She paused.

'All potential suspects, each with his or her own motive for murder.' She looked around the half-circle of faces, studying expressions. 'I don't think I've forgotten anyone . . . '

Val looked worried; had she guessed something? Wilfred moved away from Fletcher and sat with his arm around Joyce. Eyes watched her warily.

'Obviously someone has been lying,' Miss Eaton said. 'Then came the theft of a picture from Red Wheal, a big house not far from here. A valuable Gauguin, the owner claimed. Remember that Duke's bike was missing that night — and the police laboratory proved it had been in the grounds at Red Wheal.

'Sammy has admitted he rode a motor-cycle in his youth — but, of course, most people could manage it if they had to.'

Reggie Courtney looked nervous.

'I learnt that George Bullard worked as a valuer of paintings and had previously visited Red Wheal — and he claimed the Gauguin to be a worthless forgery! I wondered why a forgery would be stolen, and why only that one picture should be taken.'

Miss Eaton took another sip from her glass, and swallowed.

'Incidentally, I found the stolen picture and Inspector Reid has returned it to the owner. It seemed to me that no art thief was likely to throw a valuable painting over the cliff into the sea . . . so it had to be a forgery!'

She put Sherry on the floor and rose to

her feet. She took a palette knife from Sammy's box.

'And who do we know who can paint in the style of different modern artists?'

She turned to the demonstration painting on the easel and began to scrape away half-dry oil paint to reveal white primer and, underneath that —

As another painting began to show, Keith Parry swore and came to his feet and ran for the door.

Fletcher reached under his jacket, brought out a boomerang and threw it. The missile hit the back of Parry's head and sent him stumbling into the arms of Frank Trewin. Trewin snapped handcuffs on him.

★　★　★

After Trewin had taken Parry away, Miss Eaton sat in the Courtney's private lounge. Sherry lapped contentedly at a saucer filled with her favourite drink.

Val seemed stunned.

'It was Sherry who first made me suspicious,' Miss Eaton said. 'She doesn't take to doubtful characters, I've noticed — and she didn't like Parry at all.'

Reggie moistened his lips and looked away from his wife.

'It'll come out at the trial, I suppose. We were in it together. Not the murders — selling fake masterpieces. Keith painted them — he had a knack for what he called 'creative copying'. From my time in the art shop, I had the contacts — mostly American.

'He painted one a year — in winter, while he was staying here. Val didn't know anything about it and, of course, we got big money for them.'

'The painting of Mr. Jarvis's, I assume, was an early one?' Miss Eaton asked.

'Yes, his first attempt. That's why he felt he had to get rid of it, I suppose. It wouldn't stand up to a knowledgeable critic — as Bullard proved. And it was too close to Porthcove to take any risk after Keith killed him.

'Yes, Bullard was snooping around upstairs one day. He must have found another forgery and recognised the style of painting.'

'It was a Braque,' Reggie said dully. 'A good one.'

Miss Eaton sipped her sherry.

'So he threatened to expose Parry. I don't think he would have tried blackmail. He just liked to needle people. Possibly Parry offered him money to keep quiet. Bullard would have laughed at that. He wanted the fun of exposing someone — so Parry killed him.'

Reggie licked his lips. 'What am I going to do now?'

'Parry will talk,' Miss Eaton said briskly. 'For Val's sake, I suggest you leave the country. I shall waive my fee — after all, I'll get a substantial reward for the return of the stolen diamonds. I'm not an expert on art frauds, but I assume the police must treat it as a crime.'

Val took her husband's hand and held it tightly. 'We'll go abroad together, and make a fresh start somewhere.'

'And Joyce and Wilfred will marry and live happily ever after,' Miss Eaton said, and sighed. 'On Hilda's money.'

She put down her empty glass and picked up Sherry. 'I'll stay overnight and leave in the morning — if I'm still welcome?'

'Of course,' Val said quickly. 'I asked you to investigate. You did it for me, and St. Agatha's. You weren't to know how it would turn out.'

She began to cry, and Miss Eaton went downstairs to her room. It had been a successful case and she could look forward to seeing Gray's story in the 'Herald' yet she felt depressed.

Tomorrow she would buy the new Sam Pike novel to cheer herself up.

THE END

We do hope that you have enjoyed reading this large print book.

Did you know that all of our titles are available for purchase?

We publish a wide range of high quality large print books including:
Romances, Mysteries, Classics
General Fiction
Non Fiction and Westerns

Special interest titles available in large print are:
The Little Oxford Dictionary
Music Book, Song Book
Hymn Book, Service Book

Also available from us courtesy of Oxford University Press:
Young Readers' Dictionary
(large print edition)
Young Readers' Thesaurus
(large print edition)

For further information or a free brochure, please contact us at:
Ulverscroft Large Print Books Ltd.,
The Green, Bradgate Road, Anstey,
Leicester, LE7 7FU, England.
Tel: (00 44) **0116 236 4325**
Fax: (00 44) **0116 234 0205**

THE BLIND BEAK

Ernest Dudley

Eighteenth-century London. Blind magistrate Sir John Fielding, 'The Blind Beak', had instigated the Bow Street Runners to combat the hordes of criminals so rife throughout the city. Criminals such as Nick Rathburn, who fights his way out of Newgate Gaol. Then, by a twist of fate, Nick becomes a secret agent for 'The Blind Beak'. However, as Sir John, amid the Gordon Riots, is in the hands of the terrorising mob, Nick faces death on the gallows at Tyburn . . .

THE SECRET SERVICE

Rafe McGregor

The CIA want retired Secret Service agent Jackson back on a mission: to foil Operation Condor, a top secret plan conceived by the East German security police in the Cold War, and now in the hands of *al-Qaeda*. But he finds that he is being used as the bait in a trap. His only chance of escape is to discover who passed the plan to *al-Qaeda*. And he suspects that the answer lies in the Caribbean island of Barbados.